The Dominance Bond

The Dominance Bond

Leonard Klossner

ISBN-13: 978-0692430675

Zeit|Haus Editions are published by Zeit|Haus .
Chicago, IL

www.zeit-haus.com

The Dominance Bond

CHAPTER ONE

In which Bianca learns of her mother's death.

Bianca was tending to small pots of basil, thyme and assorted succulents arranged atop her marble kitchen table when her phone rang. She lived in a two-story apartment, and the window nearest the corded telephone that was docked on the wall of her kitchen granted her a view of a lone young elm tree in the courtyard of her residential community, the deciduous autumn leaves of which were strewn about the ground beneath the empty branches.

She had a habit of turning about-face while talking on the phone, wrapping the cord gently around her neck and down her back, so that she could peer out into the vista of the courtyard while conversing. Children often played in the grass, rode bikes in circles around the tree and gathered armfuls of fallen leaves and threw them at one another. She was fond of watching them enjoy their innocent play. At that moment, however, there was not a single child frolicking near the denuded tree. Only the fallen leaves were present, whose cracked and broken bodies covered the landscape in autumnal melancholy.

"Hello?"

She smiled unwittingly as she answered the then-unknown caller, expecting her fiancé, Thomas, to greet her.

"Good afternoon. May I speak with Bianca Schrader?"

Her expression turned serious.

"This is she."

"Good afternoon. This is Rémi Belgarde of Le Soléal."

"Yes, the cruise liner."

Le Soléal was the French cruise ship her mother and father were vacationing aboard. Her parents, both well on in years, had, some months before, outlined a shared resolution of traveling to thirty countries before the deterioration of their physical capabilities would rule it an impossibility. The country from which Rémi was calling was only ninth in the series.

Bianca wondered what occasion the crew had for calling on her. Was this standard protocol, to merely inform loved ones of the passengers' well-being?

"That is correct. I am calling from Reykjavik Iceland Cruise Port of Call. Do you have a moment?"

"Yes."

Her French intermediary spoke in a particularly dour manner which caused her heart to flutter.

"Is everything okay?" she asked.

"Well, there is not an easy way to say this but, unfortunately, your mother, Mary, passed away this morning before we could reach the port."

"She...?"

"We tried as best we could to–"

"She's dead?"

"Yes. I'm very sorry, Bianca. We tried everything we could to help her. She passed peacefully, though."

Bianca's overwhelming surprise was an emotional aegis which shielded her eyes from the intrusion of tears. She stared at the naked limbs of the elm tree for a moment, feeling for a moment that perhaps she finally understood its solitude, before gathering her wits.

"Is my father okay?"

"Yes. He is very upset, of course, but otherwise in good health."

"Is he there? Could I please speak to him?"

"I'm sorry, but he has been very busy dealing with the necessary paperwork and documents. The doctors here in Reykjavic have been very generous in receiving the body and issuing a death certificate for the deceased. We are finalizing the paperwork and will be cremating the body shortly thereafter, as your father has decided. He has expressed his desire to remain aboard the ship until it returns to France, retaining possession of the ashes."

Bianca performed another about-face so that the cord caressed her jaw and deposited itself between her lips. She began chewing the cord, compressing the spiral loop with her teeth. Her kitchen countertops were sterile and immaculate, providing a view of the tile her gaze became transfixed upon whose nondescript blankness complemented her state of mind.

"Is there any other way I could be of assistance?" Rémi asked.

"Not unless you could bring my mother back to life."

She was surprised to hear herself speak in such a way and immediately felt sorry for abusing him as she had but, despite her feelings, despite her mother's passing, despite everything, she did not apologize.

"I'm...I'm sorry, is there–"

"I suppose there's nothing we can do. Please tell my father I love him very much."

"I will do that. Again, I am very sorry for your loss. Our prayers are with you and your family at this time. Goodbye."

Bianca did not return his valediction, although, moments after hanging up, Bianca realized she had neglected to inquire about her mother's cause of death, and that Rémi had failed to provide her with the details. Mary was not so old that she could have passed without complication. She had to have fallen off of the ship, contracted a serious illness, or been the victim of a murder, Bianca thought. For a moment she imagined her father as the murderer. No, that was a role he could not play. Ray and Mary had an unconquerable friendship that the last three decades had failed to divide. If she had fallen off of the vessel, her body likely would not have been easily recovered, if it could be recovered at all, if the crew could be bothered by such efforts.

What, then, was the cause of death?

She scoured numerous international periodicals online for news involving Le Soléal but found nothing newsworthy save for an article relating the story of the Compagnie du Ponant's vessel, Le Ponant, which was seized by Somali pirates some years ago in the Gulf of Aden. If her mother's death was accomplished following the success of a biological conspirator, a fatal virus, surely she would have contracted it from a fellow passenger aboard Le Soléal, on which her mother and father had spent the last three weeks. Was that not enough time to spread the contagion among the other cruise-goers? If so, more fatalities should have followed or preceded her mother's, and was that not a news-worthy report?

It was a consequence of Bianca's despair that she inevitably surrendered to the utter lack of information, imagining a highly contagious virus as the only suitable explanation and wished for other deaths, many deaths to accompany her mother's. She could not stomach the thought of her mother dying alone. Bianca visualized a flurry of angel wings carrying the souls of the scores who she imagined had also died, each encouraging another on their ascent into Heaven, the brave among them taking the fearful spirits within their arms, lending the weak their strength so that they could all reach the gates together. Bianca imagined her mother as the bravest angel–she could not picture her any other way–whose wings spanned wider than those of the others, and whose luminescent aura lit the skyward path towards God's holy light.

She stood up to resume watering her herbs and succulents, doing so until an unknown psychological impetus triggered a spontaneous breakdown.

What was it that reminded her; the shower of droplets from the nozzle of the watering can reminding Bianca of her dormant tears, the sight of dead leaves leaving the young elm tree in the midst of winter, the temperature of the water bringing to mind the chill of the Atlantic coast?

Bianca set the watering can in its usual place atop the bookshelf that supported rows of small houseplants. She grabbed one such plant, pressing her tensed fingers against the rim of the earthen terracotta which housed it, and raised it so that it was level with her eyes. She was disgusted by the photoluminescence of its thick appendages whose lush foliage remained poised outright to receive the charity of the sun.

The profundity of the plant's suggestion of life was an insult to her mother's death. With every pound of force her trembling muscles could recruit she slammed the judge's gavel upon the sounding block, passing a cruel sentence upon the innocent shrub. Pronounced by a shrill yell, Bianca hurled the pot across the room–a sentence of death for flourishing in life. The clay pot shattered, depositing soil and clod in the grout of her kitchen tiles, and shards of cracked and shattered terracotta disabused the kitchen of its previously featureless tranquility.

She collapsed thereafter on her white suede ottoman, tucking her face into the crease between the back and bottom cushions. Her choice in material proved a prudent one as the suede deflected her every tear without complaint.

Once her eyes had ceased their incessant tribute to the departure of her mother's soul from it's body, she entered the kitchen, negotiating with the hazard of the shattered flower pot that threatened her bare feet, and poured herself a stout glass of rosé. She downed the entire bottle, which was accommodated by the capacity of three glasses, before she called Thomas.

CHAPTER TWO

Bianca, alongside Thomas, returns
to her widowed father.

Ray's health and mobility, considering his age, was excellent before his wife had passed away–of gastroenteritis, Ray confirmed when Bianca had picked him up from the airport. And, yes, a few other passengers had contracted the same bug, although the virus, like a common stomach flu, had passed in a matter of days. But due to her body's diminished capability to fight infections, and partly owing to her age, the virus succeeded in taking her life.

"God had a plan for her," Ray told his daughter. "And it's best we don't doubt it."

Ray's health had declined dramatically since his wife's death, forcing him to remain retired to bed throughout the afternoon and for the better part of the evening, although this was not a point of complaint for the old man. He was, in his younger years, more virile and energetic, naturally strong, his eyes burning with passion for his work, although the extensive passage of years had imparted upon Ray the value of rest and the virtue of inactivity. At his age, he was most comfortable behind the curtains of his closed eyes.

The old widower blamed the chill of the Scandinavian coast for stiffening his joints and casting a dark cloud over his once jovial demeanor, never admitting or even recognizing the fact of Mary's passing as though denial of her death would invalidate it, perhaps thinking she could be revived by his denial.

Thomas and Bianca, disqualifying the option of handing him over to a hospice or hiring a live-in nurse, opted to take residence in the rustic two-story home which had accommodated the Schrader family since Bianca was a child.

The lovers pulled up to the gate of her father's home. Thomas stalled the car. He placed his hand on her thigh to keep her still.

"I'll get it."

Thomas cracked scores of dead leaves beneath his boots as he walked up the cobblestone driveway to unlatch the gate, after which he returned to the car and accelerated into the driveway.

Bianca turned to her lover and sighed.

"We're finally here."

She smiled at Thomas despite her unease.

"Yeah, this is almost a sort of homecoming for you," Thomas said.

Bianca's forced laughter implied injury. Thomas wrapped his arm around her shoulders and kissed her cheek.

"Don't be worried. Everything will be fine. I know it will be hard to see your father in his current state, but it is for the best that we take care of him."

Bianca began to tear up.

Thomas took both of her hands in his and surrendered

kind condolences and promises to his wounded darling. He released her hands and placed his on the side of her neck and kissed her once more, assuring her that everything would go well. They exited the car and began removing their luggage.

"Damn fine day, idn't it?"

"Daddy!"

Bianca dropped the suitcase she had in hand and bounded over to her father. A gust of wind loosened a handful of autumn leaves from the branches covering the gloomy sky overhead.

"How is my precious little girl?"

Bianca embraced her father as though he had returned to her after years of military deployment.

"Wait a minute, why're you crying? That lousy fiancé a'yours ain't treatin' ya poorly, is he?"

Ray squinted his right eye and pantomimed with his right hand as though he were training a gun at Thomas, a sneer on his lips.

Thomas smiled and shook his head.

"Of course not, Ray."

"Cuz I tell ya I'll kill every son of a bitch that so much as brings a tear to my precious angel's eyes."

Ray embraced his daughter once again before clearing a stream of tears that the wind had blown sideways down her cheek.

"I still remember the first time you told me that," Thomas said in good humor.

"Don't believe me, boy?"

Thomas turned serious.

"I believed you then and I believe you now."

"You picked a smart one, honey."

Ray patted his daughter on her back.

"Now I suppose I can backfill that ditch I've been diggin' in the backyard."

"And I suppose I'll help you fill it," Thomas said. "I'd never do anything to earn it."

"Well, you can never be too sure of people these days, can ya? Anywho, maybe we should save it for an old man like me. Death could come visit my bedside any day now."

Bianca grasped her father's hand.

"Don't talk like that, Dad. Besides, you're in no shape to be digging, let alone standing for too long."

She spoke in an almost maternal sort of consternation, and her ignorance of her father's irony amused both men.

"Here we go, remindin' your poor old father of just how old he really is."

"But you just...look, could we please just go inside? The doctor told you that you're not supposed to be on your feet for very long."

"Doctors? Hah! Whadda they know? I tell you modern medicine is a scam. The only reason they–"

"Dad, please," whispered Bianca.

Her father's outburst colored her cheeks with a slight blush.

"You know Thomas works in medicine."

"And what does he know?"

Thomas feigned ignorance as he unloaded the last of the luggage.

"He knows much more than you and I, Dad. You should thank him for being here right now. He volunteered for this. He didn't have to, you know."

"Well, I'd be fine by myself. I don't need nobody wipin' my ass or tellin' me what's good for me. I've had seventy-two years to figure it out for myself."

"Should we go inside?" Thomas asked.

He took a moment to survey the house, old and decrepit as it was. The paint was fading from the panels, and hanging off in strips near the corners. It seemed strangely mortal to Thomas, not only alive but near the end of its life. Two windows each in a faded white frame and clouded like cataracts over eyes gazed down over the movement of the three bodies below, watching as Bianca took one suitcase and a small duffel bag while Thomas wrapped the belts of three bags and one backpack around his torso, taking the remaining suitcase in hand. Ray led them through the short walkway and up the six cement steps towards the front door, waddling up each step with a slow rhythm that was pronounced by his wheezing which followed every exhalation. Bianca looked back at Thomas and pouted over her father struggling with something that came so incredibly easy to their younger, slender bodies. Thomas' legs began to quiver as he waited below the penultimate step for Ray's shaking hands to grasp the correct key for the lock. He could not help but wonder whether Ray was playing on the disabilities of old age knowing that Thomas was burdened by such a heavy load.

"Let me help, Dad."

Ray swatted her hand and grumbled as he continued rifling through the keys. Once Ray was capable of letting them in, he explained that the couple would be taking the guest bedroom downstairs. Thomas hurried toward the room, hastening into darkness. As he hastened away, he heard Bianca raising protest over an issue which he could not determine.

Thomas searched for the light switch, running his hand along the wall until he found it. Once the room was illuminated, he found not only the bulbs of his fingers and the pad of his hand were covered in dust, but the bulb, naked and uncovered, and much of the wooden floor and panel was covered in dust as well.

He set the bags down across the bed, covering the entirety of the mattress with only four pieces of luggage which were not all grossly sizable, afterwards realizing that both he and Bianca would not be able to sleep together on this bed. It was a decisive ploy by Ray. He knew it.

Why had Mary been the one to pass? Why not her father? Thomas asked himself.

Thomas caught Bianca as he was exiting the bedroom.

"That bed is a twin. It's not big enough for both of us."

"I know," Bianca said, sighing. "My dad said we'll just need to deal with it."

"Well, I suppose I'll just sleep on the couch for the time being."

"No, Thomas, you sleep on the bed. Aren't you on call at St. Rose this week? You need to be well-rested. Besides, I'll be able to better hear if my dad's having any trouble if I sleep on the couch."

"If you insist, darling."

Thomas took her in his arms and kissed her cheeks.

"Hey now, no being vulgar in front of the Lord," Ray shouted from atop the staircase. He pointed to a framed picture of Jesus Christ hanging on a stained wooden panel of the wall.

"This may be more difficult than I imagined."

"It was your idea," Bianca joked, prodding an accusatory finger into Thomas' sternum.

"Right. Isn't it ironic how the man your father's been trying to get you to abandon is the one who suggested that we care for him?"

"Don't say that, Thomas."

She hung her head and her hair draped over her face as though to hide herself from despair.

"I don't like when you talk about my father in a bad way. Anyway, you couldn't imagine how hard I've thought about it. I love you, Thomas, and I want us to get married. I was really looking forward to starting a family with you."

Bianca struggled to control the rising tide of tears in her eyes as she spoke.

"I love you, too, Bianca, and I'm sorry. I–"

"No, don't apologize. In any case, it's better that we wait– test the waters before we commit, you know? You made me realize that there are things we need to take care of before we really begin our lives together."

As the pair made for the guest bedroom, Thomas wondered what prerequisite conditions Bianca figured needed fulfilling before they could reconfigure the course of their lives to accommodate the permanent inclusion of one another, although this thought begged questions that he considered inappropriate for the moment to ask.

"I agree. It will be difficult, but we'll be stronger for having gone through it. I just want to get along with your father."

"Oh, don't worry about that. He'll come around. He knows what a wonderful man you are. He's just jealous, that's all. I suppose he doesn't like the idea of competing with another man for my attention."

Bianca giggled.

"You know, he probably feels like you're stealing me from him."

Thomas scoffed.

"You make it seem like you're having an affair with me and that your father is the jealous boyfriend."

"You're ridiculous, Thomas. That's gross."

"Okay, fine, I'm sorry. Come here, kiddo."

Thomas wrapped her in his strong arms.

"I love you, Bianca."

She stared wistfully into his eyes.

"I love you, too, Thomas. Thank you for being here."

"Give me your tongue."

Bianca shook her head.

He gently laid her down on the bed, removed her shoes and began first massaging her feet, then licking around and between her toes and the bridges and heel of her foot.

"You're disgusting, Thomas. Stop."

"But I enjoy it. Why does it make you uncomfortable?"

"My feet have been sweating in my shoes all day. I mean, it tickles and you've already started so keep going if you want. I'm just not going to kiss you afterward."

"Don't you love me, Bianca? Wouldn't you surrender yourself to me completely to please me? I'm making such a great sacrifice being here–for you."

"Yes, I would, but some of the stuff you want to do is so disgusting, Thomas."

"Like what?"

Bianca accounted for Thomas' insistence that he indulge his mouth in her most private quarters during that rose-hued uterine drama that follows the eve of each month.

"Oh, come on. It's just blood. Didn't you ever lick at any of your wounds as a child? It just tastes like iron. You make it a much bigger deal than it is."

"No, I don't, Thomas. It's not just blood leaking from a cut. You work in a hospital. I don't need to explain menstruation to you."

Thomas shrugged and ceased massaging his lover's feet. He stood up and took a seat next to Bianca on the bed.

"You know, I think some of the morbid things you've seen at the hospital has really disturbed you. I remember you used to not be so nasty. Do you remember telling me how you went to deliver medication to a patient and when you arrived you saw that she had bled from between her legs all over the sheets? Coincidentally, I was on my period as well and you were so eager to go down on me. Remember?"

"I remember, yeah, but the incident at the hospital isn't what influenced that. I've just wanted to try it, that's all. Do you understand why I wanted to work in the medical field? Since I was young I was interested in anatomy, and I remember vividly the joy I felt from dissecting animals in middle school and having to identify the major organs, cutting and peeling back the skin without damaging the integrity of the cadaver. It's always been a fascination of mine, and I love you, Bianca, and, as your lover, I want to explore your body. Every inch of it, regardless of your condition, whether you're sweating, bleeding, and so on."

Thomas, although swept into a minor fit of passion over recollecting the discovery and cultivation of his special interests, deemed it inappropriate to repeat for Bianca the sublime pleasure experienced from being a witness to surgeons cutting into human flesh. This surgical exhibit granted Thomas a sight that the mutilation of preserved cadavers could not grant him, that being the warm gushing swell of blood draining from the incisions.

Thomas envied morticians for their unsupervised liberty over a corpse. He was jealous of the gratuitous power they could exercise over a body that could offer no resistance. Daydreams of covering a corpse in countless wounds occurred frequently in his slower hours at the hospital. When he would observe operations, he would squeeze his palms together and clench his teeth until his head would ache. At night, Thomas would lie in bed and allow fantasy the supreme license of simulating the vile deeds he would have perpetrated upon the bodies were he not accompanied by other doctors. These morbid peculiarities contributed to his paraphilias which he was largely unable to satisfy with Bianca. This was a circumstance which proved to be his paramount point of contention in their relationship, although it was one which would remain private indefinitely.

His reminiscence strong-armed him into a state of heightened arousal. He burrowed his hands between Bianca's legs and overwhelmed her face with his open mouth. Bianca thought that she was familiar enough with the nuances and idiosyncrasies of his making love to her, thus attributing his animalistic aggression to the sublimation of his anger that was born of his impotence, that his more forceful liberty with her body was his contending with psychological castration. Often he stood before an altar to which he could offer no tribute and was forced into shame like a monk having been robbed whilst on a journey to a temple at which he had designs to surrender a material sacrifice.

Theirs was often a communion only of hands and fingers, the arcane and erudite gestures of which presented a sacrament of sweat and saliva. She, jejune Bianca, did not understand that Thomas' impotence resulted from her stifling the expression of his more questionable tastes. She was additionally ignorant of the fact that he sought their satisfaction elsewhere.

In one remembered scene, taking place atop the precipice of his pleasure, she was lying on her stomach, enjoying his tender kisses and respectful, tender caresses. Thomas began to feel the warm gales of pleasure coaxing his hair to stand on end as his open mouth searched for entry into the sweet brown clove that lay enclosed between the two soft and supple sierras on her backside. When he tried to admit his tongue into its tightly sealed harem of pleasures without announcing its entrance, she shouted his name and concealed the delicious bounty hidden between the mounds of goosepimpled flesh. This angered incantation dispelled the eager swelling of his desire, leaving him frustrated and impotent.

Thomas began disrobing Bianca, placing his hand between her underwear and the soft skin of her hips.

"Bianca!" Ray shouted.

The couple shared a cocktail of consternation and regret.

Bianca surrendered her apologies to Thomas. He refused her offering.

"Just go."

She clothed herself in what little garments Thomas had managed to remove and left to find her father. The staircase leading up to the second level was covered in a thick layer of dust from disuse after the installation of a simple elevator which delivered Ray and, before her death, Mary just outside of their bedroom. The stairwell was an ornate spiral balustrade with dark polished and lacquered rails installed to match the aged and dark wooden details described throughout the rest of the home. Both ends of the staircase were crowned by wooden orbs replete with a bronze trim placed atop the flattened base of the rails.

The trim was a minor detail to which Ray had attributed the occupation of a bronze bust of Zeus in the foyer—both were bronze and a perfect match, he believed. Zeus' mythological significance was lost on Ray, who, despite his deficit of knowledge on the Greek god, excitedly recounted the story of his purchase to all and sundry as well as a fabricated history of the deity whose name he was not actually aware of, and this amused both Bianca and her mother who followed the tale by exchanging jokes behind his back. The genesis of the bust was a source of confusion for all who had bothered to ponder the matter. There were no other complementary furnishings in the house nor any other items of mythological or cultural significance.

Bianca climbed the stairs and smirked at the bust whose authoritative countenance commanded only humor considering the context of its installation.

"Yes, Dad?"

She peered into her father's bedroom, noticing after a quick inspection that it was vacant.

"Where are you?"

"In here, darlin'."

Ray fluttered a hand outside of the doorway of the room adjacent to where Bianca stood.

"What are you doing in here, Father?" she asked, shielding her eyes from the sheer brightness of the room. "You know you're supposed to be lying down."

She walked into the room and swatted at a hanging terracotta pot she had nearly run into that housed gardenias. Noticing the harness of thin twine and thread that suspended the pot, she marveled at how it continued to teeter back and forth without snapping.

Ray and Mary, having more vacant rooms than they knew what to do with, had converted the room nearest their bedroom into an indoor garden. It was Mary's idea that was met with Ray's approval following a calculated attack of jealousy after he had first denied her license to the room.

The small garden would have remained empty had Mary not occasioned to stay out late one particular night, on which, after her return, he scolded her for over an hour, demanding to know who—the name of the male—she had been with. This episode inspired Mary. Every Saturday that passed she would discuss with her husband the matter of turning the vacant room into a small garden. He denied her wish for weeks. Each time her request was denied, she would leave the house dressed in her evening's finest. Ray could only endure three weeks of this before he acquiesced, not knowing Mary was only meeting a female friend for dinner before returning home.

"God, mom sure has added to the family since I had visited last," Bianca stated.

Her mother had always referred to her plants as her children, leaving Bianca, in her youth, feeling as though she were competing for her mother's affection with a gang of houseplants, although it was a feeling whose substance was unfounded after considering the smothering brand of affection Mary would strangle Bianca with when she was not tending to her more chlorophyllic children.

"Yep. She sure has."

Ray groaned as he reached to water one of his adopted children.

"It's given me more to do to while away the time since your mother has passed, though. My thumb is old and wrinkled and not very green at my age, but I promised your mother as I held her hand hours before she passed that I would try and take care of her plants."

"That's sweet, Dad."

Bianca choked as she spoke, wiping away a few rogue tears that trespassed on the cusp of her eyelids.

"Anyway, you really shouldn't be standing as much as you have been. Maybe I could tend to Mother's garden for you."

Ray turned from the potted succulent he was watering and looked at Bianca with a sadness which was italicized by the leathern wrinkles and crow's feet on his face.

"No, Bianca," he pleaded. "Ya needa grant me this one responsibility. Besides you, all I got left is this garden. I hope ya don't think your dear old dad a loon for saying this but I sometimes talk out loud as though your mother were still alive when I'm in here. I can feel her as if she was helpin' me along, guidin' my shaking hands."

Bianca's tears expunged the faint description of liner that remained around her painted eyes following her episode when she and Thomas had arrived at the house. Black streams ran down her sun-kissed skin and collected atop the pout of her upper lip. What she did not manage to wipe away cascaded down her rosy cheeks as she spoke.

"I-I'm sorry, Dad," she stuttered over her light spastic sobbing. "Maybe Thomas and I could get you a wheelchair and you wouldn't have to stand so much."

Ray smiled, extended a shaking arm which Bianca duly moved toward, and embraced his daughter.

"I would like that very much. I can only roam about with this cane for so long. I suppose I could use your help here and there with the plants, too."

Bianca was still sobbing, her tearful moans subdued as she cried on her father's shoulder. Ray held her with both arms.

"I know it must'a hit ya pretty hard, your mother passin', and all. You couldn't imagine how much I...how much...."

Ray paused, freeing an arm to swab at his wet eyes with the dried bulbs of his plump, ashen fingers.

"I loved your mother so much. She gave me a reason to live. She was all I had–you and her was all I was livin' for. Now, you're all I got, kiddo."

"Dad," Bianca whimpered. "I don't want you to go, too."

Ray held a finger to her lips to quiet her. Bianca softened her volume.

"I just want everything to be perfect, and it's not and it won't ever be."

Bianca cleared her tears with the sleeve of her shirt.

"And you always have, Bianca," Ray said, chuckling. "Everythin' had to be in perfect order and had to happen accordin' to plan. Ya couldn't stand it any other way. I remember when I was colorin' with you when you were still so young and I put a yella crayon back in the box where you said the brown crayon was supposed to go and, boy, you started wailin', stompin' your feet and then ya tore up the picture we was workin' on together. Ya also had a tantrum over an A-minus on your report card in high school because you said the dash from the A-minus for your fourth quarter class looked so ugly. I remember you yellin' at me with tears in your eyes sayin' it wouldn't be so bad if the A-minus was for your first or sixth quarter class, but the dash in the middle made the marks on your report card look unorganized and messy. Ya weren't even upset over the lower grade. You was mad that the dash broke a pattern."

As Ray told his story, Bianca convulsed back and forth between laughing and crying.

"Let me finish waterin' these plants and we'll fix us some dinner, yeah?"

Bianca nodded. She pouted and looked up at her father like a child who implicitly entrusts all of their protection to the one they so gaze upon, the tears in her eyes making her blue irises shine like moonlight upon a lonesome sea.

Just as Ray raised the watering can to water the gardenias that were still rocking from when Bianca had swatted at them earlier, using one of his shaking hands to resist the plant's rocking motion, he let it down to turn and respond to the knocking at his bedroom door.

"In here, boy."

Thomas probed his head in and surveyed the room from left to right, cautious of offending with his presence.

"I hope I'm not disturbing anything."

"Speak, boy."

Instead of addressing what he had come up to speak to Bianca of, he turned to her, noticed her tears and asked her what was wrong, finally entering the room to take her into his arms and kiss the tears from her shuttered eyelids. Ray watched the couple from his peripheral, although he turned to tend to the flowers when his eyes had briefly caught Thomas'.

"It's nothing," Bianca answered.

She grasped Thomas' hands.

"We were just reminiscing about Mother. I'm fine. What were you going to say?"

"Oh, just that I would be happy to start dinner if everyone is hungry."

"How are ya gonna fix dinner when ya don't even know what's in the house?" Ray asked.

Thomas smirked.

"I've already taken a look. I was thinking stuffed bell peppers."

"That sounds great, Thomas," said Bianca.

"So, I'll get started, then?"

Thomas left before an answer could be given.

"I'll be down in a minute, honey," Bianca called out.

She turned to her father.

"He's perfect, isn't he?"

Ray disregarded her question with a dismissive wave of his hands.

"Give him a break, Dad. You said you always wanted me to find a strong, supportive man who would take care of me and keep my best interests before his, and I've found all of those things in Thomas. We're all living in the same house now so please try to get along. He's been nothing but nice to you."

"Go help the boy with dinner."

Ray's tone was as blunt as he could manage.

"I'm going to lie down for a bit. Wake me up when everythin's ready, will ya?"

His frustrated daughter sighed as she walked away and waved her hand.

"Sure, Dad."

Bianca entered the kitchen, and Thomas turned to welcome her with a smile.

"God, bell peppers?"

"What's wrong? They sounded great to you a minute ago. What did Ray say to you?"

"Nothing. Don't get me wrong: I'll eat them, but—I was just thinking about it—they smell so awful when they're cooked."

The two argued over petty details until Thomas addressed her father's impatience, impersonating him complaining about the meal being prepared.

Bianca suppressed a laugh and slapped Thomas on the shoulder.

"You're terrible."

"You agreed to marry me. What does that say about you?"

"I guess that makes me a fool, doesn't it?"

"That's it. You asked for it."

Thomas grabbed a handful of the raw stuffing left over from the prepared batch and shoved it in Bianca's face.

"Mmf…Thomas. Stop!"

"Quiet, or we'll have your dear old dad yelling down at us again. Now apologize for what you said."

"Never," she yelled.

Thomas clasped his hand around her mouth.

"I told you once, Bianca. Don't make me tell you again."

"What if I do it again on accident? What are you going to do?"

Bianca had barely managed to finish asking before she squealed in laughter as Thomas poked his fingers into her sides.

She begged hysterically through his hand which he kept clasped to her mouth for him to stop. Thomas ignored her and wrestled her to the floor. He moved his free hand from her hips and down her legs, her shorts falling under its gentle sweeping.

"What are you doing, Thomas? My father is upstairs."

"Just be a good little girl and keep quiet. He won't find us out if you'd stop being so damn noisy."

He licked his fingers and then started leafing them around her delicate little feminine flower, whispering vulgarities into her ear while she draped an arm over her eyes, gasping as she moaned hushed replies to his sexual inquiries.

"Who's Daddy's perfect little girl?"

"You're so nasty, Thomas."

Bianca's moaning defied her condemnation.

Thomas kept on, encouraging Bianca in her role as his

daughter.

"I love you, Thomas. I love you."

Her hips gyrated against her lover's hand in rhythm with her intonation.

Thomas ran his other hand through her hair like a loving father and kissed her face, her lips, her neck, and tongued her ear.

"I love you," he whispered.

He shifted his mouth over the lobe of the opposite ear.

"My little Binky Baby."

Bianca gasped in supreme pleasure. Her half-nude body shuddered in orgasm.

Binky Baby was Bianca's nickname her father had given her as a toddler. It was inspired, first, by her refusal to surrender her pacifier well past the recommended age and, second, for the epithet's similitude to Bianca. She had aged eight years until she had finally given up her binky. She went to school with it in her pocket, taking frequent bathroom breaks and secluding herself in corners of the schoolyard to suck on it in secret, and she would fall asleep and wake up with her pacifier still in her mouth.

Bianca opened her eyes following her orgasm and noticed Thomas grinning. He slowed his thrusting, and she observed, with curiosity partially distracted by the pleasurable aftershock of her climax, Thomas eyeing his penetrating member with enthusiasm. She contracted her abdominal muscles and sat up, supporting her body with her elbows. Thomas' penis was covered in blood. She squirmed a few inches away, revealing a small puddle that had formed beneath her, and this small body of reddish moisture was like a gulf of blood that had been cast between the two. A drop fell from Thomas' glans and splattered on the floor.

Thomas crawled over Bianca and attempted to reinsert his

penis, but Bianca barred him entry with her hands. Thomas grunted and struggled with her protesting limbs, finally pinning them to her sides while he forcefully negotiated with her canal that had tightened during his momentary absence. The blood lubricated his member and sloshed between thrusts. Tears returned to her eyes which had recently become so fond of sadness. Thomas knew her tears were not a denial of consent, although he was certain that she was no longer enjoying the sex. Thomas admired her for her sacrifice, offering her sex wound to her lover. His thrusting had churned the blood into a paste which had dried rapidly. The penetration began to hurt Bianca. Still she fought against her pain for her lover's sake. Desire swelled and pulsated madly in Thomas' engorged member. He shut his eyes and imagined finishing inside of her, lathering the bloody cream until he had softened completely, edging himself nearer to orgasm. But Bianca pressed her knees into Thomas' abdomen and pushed him away.

"What the fuck, Bianca?"

Thomas tried to crawl onto Bianca once again.

"Get off of me."

"I'm right there," Thomas said, caressing himself, his strokes dragging against the skin of his penis due to the dry menstruation.

"I don't care. I don't want you. I'm done."

"Let me finish. I'm right there."

His desire was diminishing. Thomas hurried his strokes so he would not become soft.

"No."

Bianca stood up and made her way to the kitchen counter, grabbing a half-dozen sheets of paper towels, and wet them in the sink.

"Look at the mess you've made."

"That I made? It came from your body."

"So what? I don't care. It's so disgusting that you would fuck me while I'm bleeding."

"But you let me."

"Well, I shouldn't have."

"What's your problem, Bianca? Why are you being like this?"

"You and I just like different things. We are not sexually compatible."

Thomas, recognizing the truth of her statement, hesitated for a few moments before attempting to dissuade her that that was not the case.

"It's true and you know it," Bianca said.

Bianca bent over to grab her clothes, her back turned to Thomas. She revealed the swollen lips of her vagina and the rosebud of her ass that had collected a rosy ring of blood around the orifice. Thomas stroked himself while his eyes travelled down the dried stream of blood that had trailed down her legs.

Bianca placed her clothes on the kitchen table and used the remaining moistened paper towels to wipe the blood from between her legs. Thomas continued to stroke himself.

"I'm going to cum."

Bianca turned around.

"What?"

Thomas continued to stroke himself.

"Why are you masturbating?"

"You got to have your orgasm. Why can't I have mine?"

"You're disgusting."

"Let me finish on your ass."

"No. What the hell's wrong with you? Go in the bathroom."

"Babe, please. Let me finish on your ass before you put your clothes on. Please."

Bianca groaned.

"Fine."

She bent over the counter and sashayed her hips lazily. Thomas intermittently paused his stroking to rub the head of his newly engorged penis against the cheeks of her ass until he finally achieved climax. The abatement of his desire and its diminished return contributed to a meager load of transparent mucus that dripped onto Bianca's skin. Thomas could not enjoy the subsequent pleasure that generally follows an orgasm with a partner before he was overwhelmed with shame. He regretted being so insistent.

Bianca turned around and trained a hateful look on him.

"Are you happy now?"

She cleaned the mucus from her skin and proceeded to dress herself. Never before had Thomas felt so emotionally distant from Bianca.

"My God. Thomas, what is that?"

He stopped. The musk of burnt matter was faint for just a moment before it overwhelmed him.

"Oh, goddammit, I burnt the dinner."

The oven bellowed black fog once he opened the door, and Thomas hurried to retrieve the smoking baking sheet and throw it onto the stovetop.

"Now what are we going to do?" Thomas asked.

"You're asking me? You're the master chef."

"Well, aren't you just so goddamn smart?"

Thomas' playacting was injected with the venom of his sudden antipathy towards her.

"And you're so easily hurt. Where did the strong man I was to marry go off to? I could have sworn he was here a second ago."

But where had the sweet, cherubic woman he knew in Bianca flown off to? She had never once spoken to him in such a condescending manner. Her humor, like her fiancé's, costumed her momentary hatred towards her partner.

The disappeared man, thought Thomas, who was then confined to obsessive patterns of worry, was never there. It was only the short statured frame of a sick, maladjusted wretch standing in the shadow cast by a man poised with confidence and self-assuredness. The Thomas Bianca knew was a figure unrecognizable to himself, as was the woman Bianca seemed to have become; she was a character unknown. It was as though, through some arcane sexual alchemy, they had each been transmuted into elements that became further removed from their original properties and could no longer interact with one another.

"You and your father can eat scorched bell peppers. I'm going to go out if this is how I'm going to be treated."

"So sensitive," Bianca said. "Here, let me kiss those tears. I was just joking."

Taking Bianca in his arms, he stole a kiss from her open mouth. He felt that he was kissing Bianca, or Bianca insofar as he once knew her, farewell before the spirit of the woman she once was disappeared forever.

"Luckily for you, so was I."

"Luckily for me, huh?" Bianca said, smirking. "In what way?"

"You're lucky that I don't leave you."

"You? Leave me? You wouldn't dare."

"Well, we'll just have to see about that."

Thomas was grateful for his ability in emotional mimicry, the faculties from which he could effectively pantomime confidence, for his words were not imparted with authentic assuredness. In a manner of good humor, Thomas deflected his underlying fear of abandonment by seeking to project it onto Bianca, who bore it in full form like a sheet stretched to almost unbearable dimensions to accommodate the physical scope of a visual projection. Indeed, they unknowingly shared each other's greatest fear: that of one deceiving the other, with Thomas' fear developing because of the satisfaction he often could not give her.

He, with increasing obsessiveness, imagined her with a myriad of men–first with lovers from her past (shadowed figures serving to complete the illustration were one's particular likeness not known to Thomas). Then she was cast with men with whom she was previously acquainted. In the final stage of his secret obsession, Thomas would project an imagined representation of a man he would notice in any odd place into making love with Bianca whether she were alongside Thomas at that moment or not.

Following these imagined trysts Thomas forced Bianca into by way of his mad worry, Thomas would play himself, naturally, as the deceived lover who each time discovered his love enwrapped and enraptured by another man.

These fantasies would forever remain a secret. He would not even admit to himself that his jealous imaginings were suffused with a sense of pleasure. These fevered daydreams would at once serve as an affliction and its remedy; in one throe bolstering his repressed rage and, in another, relieving his angry pressure through dreamed scenes of torture and murder of the men he cast into the cerebral dramas to cuckold him.

It could be stated by all accounts that Bianca had treated their relationship with the utmost fidelity, but, to Thomas, what with the passions he had devoted to his obsession, she had done as well as to deceive him, although he was not allowed the supreme explosive expression granted those who have knowingly been scorned by their lovers as his betrayal was a hypothetically entertained affair. Thomas dared not speak a word of his worry owing to a fear that was not unlike that which one who refuses to visit the doctor keeps–an anxious concern that their fear will be validated in the revelation of their developing the very disease they worried they may have had all along. Thomas would prefer to ignore and die unwittingly from his suspicions than to have them confirmed.

"Yeah, I suppose we will have to see about that," Bianca said.

Her brow was tensed above angry eyes which were fixed on Thomas.

"As for dinner, maybe we could just have some grilled cheese," Thomas said.

"Have you ever considered quitting medicine? I think the culinary arts is your strong suit."

"You know, what am I going to do when the woman I fell in love with becomes too much to bear?"

He retained the image of his recent sexual frustration in the rear chambers of his memory as he spoke.

"Are you getting sick of me, Thomas?"

"Not yet, darling."

Thomas turned to Bianca. The bare skin exposed through her shirt at the nape of her neck was all he could intimate of her flesh. She stood, back turned, before the kitchen counter, tending to nothing in particular, unable to see Thomas smiling at her.

CHAPTER THREE

Thomas finds himself at odds with
Bianca and her father.

The weeks in which Thomas and Bianca argued over the old man's lot–whether he should be given up to clinical care or granted his daughter's care with Thomas' assistance– were a gauntlet of trials for the pair. One week they decided Ray would be handed over to a local hospice. The following week they agreed he should be administered the couples' care. In their negotiations over Bianca's sick father their relationship itself became terminal. The rhythm of their hearts escaped synchronization and, owing to the silence in the pumping of their warm blood, their hearts, encased behind flesh and bone, secretly throbbed in contempt for one another.

Mary passed away four weeks before Thomas and Bianca's October wedding. Ray and his wife were to return home from their Scandinavian cruise a week before the wedding, shaking

hands and embraces with the dearest members of Thomas'
family. Now, the union was ruined. It was a fault attributed to
no one, merely a tragic quirk of circumstance.

Thomas was rather fond of Mary. His own parent, the only
one that had not fled, was eccentric and irrational, spending
weeks abroad and designating his care to relatives in the most
formative years of his youth, and was less of a mother to
Thomas than Mary seemed. He had wept for Mary's passing.
Never once did he cry when his mother died.

Bianca, naturally, was easily irritated and short with
Thomas, yet demanded from him an attention to emotional
detail which he could not easily spare. Considered, they could
not maintain close proximity for long before their nerves, frayed
so easily when in each other's company, rendered their present
dinner a tense affair. This tension was escalated by the presence
of Bianca's possessive father.

Ray waddled with a labored and uneven gait into the
kitchen.

"Why's it smell like my goddamn house is on fire?"

Thomas, poring over the new course he was preparing,
muttered curses under his breath.

"My breathing's bad enough already. Ya tryin'a give me
emphysema?"

You deserve worse, old man, thought Thomas.

"Thomas burned the dish he was preparing," Bianca
explained. "So no more stuffed bell peppers."

Thomas' silence towards Bianca and her father unnerved
her. She knew there was a latent violence in his silent demeanor.
Despite how heated a number of their verbal arguments had
been, his silence denoted a morbid rage in which Thomas
entertained detailed and gratuitous fantasies of harming the
offenders. He had admitted this fancy to Bianca after she
was, only once, the recipient of such treatment. Her offense:

confessing to a dream she had wherein she made love to a former suitor.

The abstraction of dreams and the psychoanalytic faculties employed to interpret them, since—and Thomas knew this—dreams cannot be interpreted literally, in this case, were of no consequence to him. Due to his frenzy, all reason had been disposed of by jealousy. Thomas' logic in that episode was defined by this consideration: Bianca still thought of a former lover. This recognition created thought patterns which were like a maze through which Thomas hopelessly stumbled in search of what those romantic dreams fulfilled for her that he did not.

Thomas set three bowls of macaroni and silverware on the table, placing Ray's in front of him without so much as an offensive gesture.

"What is this?" Ray asked.

"Southwestern macaroni and cheese—bacon, cheese, bits of the bell peppers I could salvage."

"There ya go makin' me feel young again, boy," Ray said, chuckling as he spoke. "My mother used to make this for me all the time growin' up. Tell me, boy, am I going to get a toy with my meal?"

"Dad, stop."

Thomas looked Ray dead in the eye.

"Oh, it's nothin'. Just a little fun between men. Isn't that right, boy? Everyone needs a good ribbin' once in a while."

I can't wait to watch you wither away.

Thomas did not divert his eyes from Ray's for a moment.

Your daughter wouldn't get to hear you choke on your last words if it were up to me, you old bastard.

"I think I hurt his feelings," Ray said.

He manipulated his face into numerous comic expressions to tease Thomas. As he refused to react, Ray continued badgering him.

"Yep, I hurt his feelings."

He laughed, patted both of his hands on his stomach and laughed, feeling pleased with himself for angering his daughter's fiancé.

"Dad, please."

"Well, it was good clean fun 'til your fiancé here started lookin' like he'd like to take me out back. Whaddya say, boy? Wanna put on some gloves and do a number on this old man?"

"I'd like to do much worse to you."

Thomas was shocked to hear himself having spoken out loud.

"Thomas!"

Ray, meaning to pardon himself, struggled to help himself up.

"Well, there's nothing left to say about that. I am going back upstairs. Would you mind carrying my plate, Bianca?"

"Of course not, Dad."

She trained a pair of hateful eyes on Thomas.

"Watch your future husband and make sure the boy doesn't spike my IV with arsenic."

Ray chuckled as Bianca helped him to his feet, satisfied with his victory.

"I'm really sorry, Dad."

"Don't apologize for the boy. A real man would take responsibility for himself."

Ray departed past the corner into the foyer. Bianca followed her father, first turning to look at Thomas. She scowled at him before rounding the corner and ascending the groaning wooden staircase whose darkness soon consumed them both.

"Believe me, we'll have a good, long talk about it," Bianca's distant voice echoed.

Thomas' imaginings delivered he and Ray into a torture chamber, a coliseum in which reincarnated Ray, revived after being violently dispatched, was forced to face a series of assailants, bound to a table or chair depending on the artist's taste for the scene, intermittently being momentarily transposed into an empty warehouse in which he was bound and restrained.

First, he was a prisoner of war under interrogation by rebel soldiers. Instruments of torture were assorted atop a wooden table. He shouted extorted confessions amidst his brutal torture which his abductors wrote down and recorded before finally decapitating the bastard. In another fantasy, Ray, strolling along the streets of New York at dusk, found himself a helpless target of indiscriminate gang violence. He was cornered and mugged. The perpetrators spat fluids and racially-charged hate speech before stomping his head in, leaving brain matter and other gore flecked on the street.

Bianca signaled her return to the kitchen with a violent pronunciation of her fiancé's name.

"What in God's name has gotten into you?"

Thomas pursed his lips and shrugged.

"Seriously, what evil spirit is living inside of you? He's sick, Thomas. I absolutely will not let you talk to my father like that."

Thomas remained dispassionate.

"Can you not see how incredibly hateful he is towards me? I am sure that you could be yelling at me with tears in your eyes telling me it's over and throwing the ring off of your finger and he would be standing, or, you know, lying down upstairs in his deathbed smiling. He'd be so happy to be getting his little girl back all to himself. Then you would be in tears and he would take you in his arms and act so goddamn sympathetic when he couldn't really care less. He would be smirking at me behind your back. You know he wants me gone more than anything."

"Well, what's the point of all of this if my own father doesn't like anything about you?"

"Oh, come on, Bianca. Don't be like this. I understand

that you're angry but be rational, please. I must be the only one who remembers when your dad was once actually cordial and respectful towards me. This, of course, was before I proposed. That ring ruined it all. You know it's jealousy. Do you remember telling me that I reminded you of your father? This was before I even met the guy."

"That doesn't excuse the way you acted towards my sick father whose wife has just passed."

"Fine. You know what? You're right. I'm sorry. His behavior doesn't justify mine, but all I ask for is a little patience and understanding as patience is all I've had for him. Does he even know moving in to keep him company was my idea, that I was the one who convinced you?"

"I understand where you're coming from but I'm still mad at you. What you said was...how could you speak to my father like that? I'd like you to sleep on the couch tonight."

"It's not like I have much of a choice. There's no room for me on the bed, anyway."

"Goodnight, Thomas."

"Bianca, I'm sorry."

Silence. Absence. Lights switched off. A flannel blanket on the couch provided adequate warmth. Thomas made himself comfortable and returned to his reserved front-row seat in his mental coliseum in which Ray was the repeatedly resurrected combatant. Thomas was the final victor, standing up from his seat, stepping down to the coliseum floor, and murdering Ray, ending his spell of reincarnation. Bianca, furious over her father's murder at her fiancé's hands, demanded a divorce. Her Roman tears afforded Thomas a sadistic smile that remained until the last of his waking moments.

CHAPTER FOUR

To Bianca, a promise is made.

Against her, a betrayal is committed.

"Where are you off to?" Bianca asked.

"I'm off to discuss the terms of our divorce with my lawyer, dear."

"That's not funny, Thomas. I'm still mad at you."

"You won't be for long."

Thomas' smile was received and returned as confusion by Bianca.

Thomas realized long ago that he could manipulate Bianca through his issuing commands. A past exchange stands as perfect evidence.

Dramatis Personae

Thomas - *pharmacy technician, engaged to* Bianca, *aged twenty-eight*

Bianca - *Engaged to* Thomas, *aged twenty-six*

Asja - Thomas' *former love, aged twenty-two*

The action takes place at dusk in Bianca's apartment.

SCENE

A quaint living room illuminated by a lamp in the north-east corner, white drapes covering two windows, between which is situated a white suede ottoman. Thomas *returns from the hospital after a twelve-hour shift. Succulents are neatly arranged atop a marble table and the black wooden shelves of a renovated bookshelf. The blinds are drawn, the floors swept, the table and shelves tidy. The muted drone of a dishwasher hums in the background.*

(Thomas *removes his jacket, hanging it from the brass coat rack to the left of the front door*)

Bianca: We need to talk, Thomas.

Thomas: Good evening to you, too, Bianca.

Bianca: I'm not kidding. I met up with Desiree earlier today at Rakeman's Deli. She tells me she saw you and Asja having a night out last week.

(Thomas *takes off his shoes, administers a pair of cedar shoe trees to their interior and takes great care to set them side by side in the closet adjacent to the front door*)

Bianca: What do you have to say for yourself?

(Thomas *approaches the white suede ottoman and lies down*)

Thomas: Well, she isn't wrong, necessarily.

Bianca: What is that supposed to mean?

Thomas: I knew you wouldn't understand if I told you. You would assume I was being unfaithful.

Bianca: Yeah, that's what I've been thinking, Thomas.

(Thomas *sits up–straight posture–and clasps his hands, looking Bianca in the eye*)

Thomas: I was away for an hour. This much you know. Look....

(Thomas *stands up to remove his wallet from the rear pocket of his pants; sits back down*)

Thomas: I still have the receipt for the steak and wine, proving we dined and nothing more. Note the time on the receipt. Now, remember that I returned home not long after.

Were an objective show of evidence not the goal of this presentation, perhaps then fitting mention could be made of Thomas' ingenuity in coordinating a tryst with Asja with the assistance of his easily manipulated friend, Paul. Paul and his mother, well on in her years, cordially dined together once a week in the later afternoon of each Tuesday. Paul, after chauffeuring his mother home, would meet at a café which was equidistant from Thomas' studio apartment.

An exchange: Paul's dinner receipt for Thomas' hearty thanks and feelings of indebtedness, although they were not followed by an attempt at any sort of repayment, but all of this is beside the point.

Let us now return to the act we abandoned, finishing the scene in prose.

"It doesn't matter," Bianca said. "How do I know you guys didn't at least kiss? I know you used to love her, Thomas. I can't trust you anymore. You've ruined everything. It's over."

Bianca was sincere and would not have wavered if Thomas were not wise to a psychological impetus to control, a circuitous shortcut skipping over all logic and reason that assaulted her emotions exclusively.

Thomas chuckled.

"You don't mean it."

"Yes, I do, Thomas. You can't be trusted."

"Bianca, you're my baby. I know you. My little girl couldn't mean such strong words."

He fidgeted with a small coin he had taken from his pocket for a few moments.

"You don't mean it."

He spoke with certainty as if he had read her mind and composed himself with such certainty. Bianca's statements were manipulated into inauthenticity through the issuance of a command–she did not mean it for he had convinced her that she did not. He had willed it so. One day following their split, she later found herself in his company after earlier finding his absence nearly intolerable. She had almost left free, then, to the world, but she was his and his only, bound to him through subtle mechanisms of control.

Now, let the narrative return to the scene at the outset of this chapter.

"I am off to see Paul for breakfast."

"How do I know you're not off to see Asja?" she groaned. "God, we should just get a divorce."

"Don't be so impatient, darling. We aren't married just yet." Thomas smirked.

"I'm glad this is fun for you," Bianca yelled. "But this is killing me. Take your ring back. Give it to that bitch, Asja."

Before Bianca could remove her ring, Thomas, seated on the couch while in the midst of tying his shoes, rose, with shoes untied, to his feet. He took Bianca's hands in his and shifted his tone immediately into one of seriousness.

"Now you're being irrational. I promised you I would never see Asja again. We're engaged now and, once we figure things out, we will be getting married. Your ring is my promise that I will never love another woman but you for the rest of my life. I swear to you that Paul and I are going out for breakfast and a round at the shops. What Asja and I had is over. I swear to you."

"Okay, Thomas."

She was blushing.

"Don't worry."

Thomas kissed an orphan tear that was abandoned by the

other which ran down her face.

"Anyway, I plan on making a purchase that will benefit the both of us."

"What is it?"

"You will just have to wait and see, my love. Also, I'd like you to be ready for a night on the town when I get back. I've made reservations at Caneletto's."

"Caneletto's? What a gentleman, even though you're an asshole."

"Such is the nature of this beast."

Thomas kissed Bianca on her blooming cheeks and bid her farewell.

Thomas, especially after what had happened last night, was beginning to regret opting to move into Ray's home. He wished they would have agreed to leave him at a hospice, but the situation was not without its advantages. Ray's neighborhood was nearer Asja's flat.

He stepped outside, filling his lungs with air free from the dust and doom of the gloomy house, and boarded the taxi he had called for.

Asja answered the door wearing a large floral print blouse whose ruffles frolicked just below the lovely throat that Thomas could not help but wet with his kisses before any words were offered. The colorful semi-translucent fabric rested gently on the humble summit of her shoulders and thrust out over the contours of her generously proportioned breasts like the violent burgeoning crash of a waterfall, the point after which the blouse hung loose and waved gaily at the breeze that coaxed it into a modest dance. Her gaunt bones framed the full open pout of her lips.

Asja's refined sexual ardor forced Thomas to exercise a nearly impossible measure of self-control. A whiff of her perfume coerced him into poorly masked fits of fidgeting and his teeth would clench almost habitually as he fantasized about and obsessed over thoughts of taking Asja by the neck and taking her tongue over and around his, sucking her sweet saliva into his mouth and spitting it all back into hers after she would admonish him for touring his hands across the finer features of her body before she deemed it appropriate.

Thomas would surrender himself to pure primality when Asja would present her body to him, an occasion which Asja eagerly awaited each time Thomas visited, a hidden desire she would not confess to lest she surrender the ruse of feminine authority with which she spited his natural struggle for dominance.

The way he made love to Asja was overwhelming, suffocating, and claustrophobic. He kissed her in ways he had never kissed Bianca. He wanted to hurt her like a child who adores a pet so much that they threatened to break their bones while embracing them. He loved to squeeze her until she was gasping for air, sticking his fingers into her mouth and using her saliva to sully her make-up; additionally fond of lying atop her, compressing her lungs as they commingled.

Thomas greeted his mistress. Asja smiled and returned his salutation. It was bright in her home, warm and comforting, naturally lit at that hour by sunlight. She took him by the hand and let him in. The back porch door was open, letting in a cool draft. Jazz was playing from the stereo. He reached to place his hand over her cheek, a gesture she deflected with a slap on his arm.

"Not yet."

"I can't be away for very long. Let me take you now."

It was absolute that he seek Asja's permission.

"You are so like a child, Thomas—a child who cries because he can't just yet open a toy his mother has promised to purchase for him. If you have more important plans then please feel free to go."

"Don't be ridiculous."

Thomas' heart was seized with anxiety and beat hard against his chest as he spoke.

"You know I want you more than anything, ever. Always.

"More than your fiancée, Thomas?"

He nodded.

"Say it."

Thomas spoke without hesitation.

"I want you more than her."

"No, say her name."

"I want you more than Bianca."

"What are you thinking about doing to me, Thomas?"

"Too much, Asja. Everything Bianca won't let me do to her."

Thomas began bouncing his leg.

"She won't let me choke her. I can never go down on her when she's...."

"Relax. Let me pour you a drink."

"Thanks, but just one. If I don't get my hands on you soon I'll end up on the front page of the paper and behind bars."

Asja cracked a smile. She poured Thomas a drink as he stood to remove his jacket.

"Isn't that the jacket Bianca bought you?"

"Yes."

Thomas was confused, his puzzlement arising over the reason for Asja's asking. She was only interested in details of his relationship with Bianca insofar as particular actions and gestures further betrayed him against her. This time, he learned, was no different. Asja, as Thomas' former love, took pleasure in spiting the woman who had stolen her lover away.

"Keep it on. I want you to fuck me in it."

The glass containing Thomas' cocktail was bedecked with countless droplets that had culminated in a circular puddle on the surface of Asja's table by the time they concluded their encounter. Thomas fixed his lapel and smiled in amusement at Asja, who had draped her blouse solely over her breasts and laid with her arm outstretched over the bridge of her nose.

"What happened to you?" Thomas asked.

"I'm miserable. You hurt her."

"She knew what she was getting herself into."

"She's swollen, Thomas."

Asja, despite her injury, nonetheless caressed her sex.

"Well, I smell like your cunt, Asja. What are we going to do about that?"

"That's your problem. My problem is that I can't walk without pain right now."

"I'm glad you had a good time."

Asja scoffed.

"Go away. Get out of here. I hate you."

Thomas went to wash his genitals in her bathroom sink, after which he left without saying another word, enjoying the faint tremors of sexual pleasure following the satisfaction of a routine for the nth time.

CHAPTER FIVE

Thomas reveals his views regarding marriage
to Paul, and finds himself once
again in Bianca's favor.

"We're getting a divorce," Thomas told Paul.

"Are you serious? Why? What happened?"

Paul was short with dull, ruddy skin. His ugliness suggested the passing of two decades more than he had aged. He was reliable, though, often despite himself, and Thomas valued his friendship for this paramount reason. Without Paul's complicity, Thomas would not be allowed as many trysts with Asja as had been granted him. The weekly meal receipt was his saving grace. Paul's mother was Thomas' double in the operation, his stand-in. But Paul's involvement did not come without exacting a toll on his insipid conscience. He acted despite his guilt as Bianca's deceiver due to a craving for Thomas' approval. Paul failed himself on the evening of each Tuesday but succeeded in his deceptive role for Thomas' sake, never requesting any sort of recompense. Thomas' affirmation was a perfect reward.

"No, I'm joking. I know that, were she to find out about Asja and I, she still wouldn't dare. I mean the world to her."

Thomas hailed the taxi he had ordered from the only cab company in town whose fleet included pick-up trucks. The driver assisted the two friends with securing a mattress and matching box spring to the wide bed of his truck. Once the mattress was secured, Thomas bowed slightly in thanks, thinking the Korean driver was not quite fluent in English, and, after climbing into the cabin of his truck, gave him directions to Ray's house.

"But doesn't she mean the world to you?" Paul asked as he climbed in.

"I love the sex Asja and I have, but I don't love her. On the other hand, my sex life with Bianca is not much to speak of, yet I can't help but love the bitch."

"How, uh...why are you getting married, then? If you're just...you know...well, if you're cheating on her?"

"Security, Paul. Marriage is a socioeconomic construct. Maybe an outdated one at that, nowadays. In many cultures and in days past marriages were arranged, a means of two wealthy families to combine their wealth. A woman couldn't hope to amount to anything if their family did not arrange for her to marry a man of wealth. Bianca speaks out from time to time, but she's easily controlled. She'll never leave me."

There was an element of fear pervading Paul's friendship with Thomas, arising from something that Paul was too worried to look inside of himself to identify. Paul had never stopped to question how and when Thomas had come to put him under his control, but that was owing to it having happened against his wits. Paul, in his relationship to Thomas, was like one who wakes up to find blood on his bedsheets but fails to locate a wound.

Thomas' ultimate statement gave Paul cause for grave consideration: *She'll never leave me.* Paul, though he would be loath to admit it, realized the same could be said for him: he was easily controlled. He would never leave Thomas. Thomas had sunk his teeth into Paul, but Paul was thankful for the scars, grateful to be branded, to belong to somebody.

Paul almost never agreed with Thomas, but his protestations were gentle. The manner in which they were posed were searching for affirmation: *But Bianca would be upset if she were to find out, wouldn't she?*

Paul's engagement in such a discussion was like an innocuous youth finding himself accidentally at odds with the schoolyard bully. After being swept into the spirit of the moment, he throws a pulled punch which almost fails to connect and grazes the bully's chin. Realizing thereafter what he has done, and what he is in for, he then apologizes profusely for fear of severe reprisal.

"But she's so sweet, so pretty," Paul said. "How could you do that to her? What would she think if she found out that you felt that way?"

Thomas never grew impatient with Paul's questioning him as it gave him the opportunity to expound on the rationale behind his thoughts and actions.

"First of all, she will never know any of this unless, of course, you tell her, and I know that you won't. Lastly, it isn't my business what she, or anyone, thinks about anything. There is no good business in anyone's thoughts outside of my own."

"You don't even care about what your wife thinks? You don't value her input at all?"

"My fiancée, you mean."

Paul apologized.

The taxi arrived at the house.

"You can just pull up right to that gate," Thomas told the driver.

"Anyway," Thomas went on. "Think about it: how are you able to see me, or anything else, right now?"

"Because, um," Paul hesitated. "My eyes."

He spoke as though he were asking for Thomas' confirmation.

"Well, yeah. Sure, but where do those lead to?"

"The brain?"

"Sure. Now, how are you able to nervously tap your fingers against your thumb like you just did?"

"Because...I don't know. This stuff you're saying about Bianca, it's just...."

"Look, how are you able to process images, sounds, sensations, emotions? How are you able to look at that over there and realize it's a two-story brick house with six windows facing the street, one of them through which you can see my fiancée carelessly undressing?"

Paul blushed and could not manage an answer.

"Don't be nervous, Paul. She has a nice body, doesn't she?"

Paul nodded but was embarrassed to have done so.

"So what is it, Paul?"

"What's what?"

"You never answered my question."

"Yes...yeah. I nodded. I agree."

"You agree?"

"Yes."

"Agree with what?"

"She has...that she has a, um...a nice body."

"No, you idiot."

Paul cringed, and the sight of Paul's sour expression amused Thomas.

The driver began loosening the ropes that bound the mattress and box spring to the bed of his truck, refusing the assistance offered by Thomas and Paul.

"Go back to the first question."

"Oh, right."

Paul scratched the back of his head and chuckled nervously.

"Well, I don't know. Because of your brain, right?"

"Right, because of my brain."

Thomas prodded at his own temple to emphasize his point.

"None of this would exist anymore if not for this. If I were to die, it would be 'Goodbye, Bianca,' 'Goodbye, Paul,' and 'Goodbye, I,' and so long to everything else, even the concept of existence itself. What is all of this if not a series of mentally designated images that common perception agrees is universal? Who are those in agreement? Are they forms simulated by my mind, speaking a language crafted by my tongue and stylized by my hand? Maybe I as a conceptualized entity do not exist outside of my brain's electrical impulses, meaning the same for you, and everyone else for that matter. All nebulae, all galaxies, the planets and stars, all lifeforms, even the gods, bow to my sentience. When I pass, so, too, do they."

"Thomas, I think you've had too much to drink."

Thomas wrapped his arm around Paul's shoulder and laughed.

"There's no such thing. Anyway, what do you think?"

"Maybe you have."

Paul's volume was as soft as refined cotton.

"No, what do you think about what I just said?"

"I'm not too sure. I've never thought about it. I mean, as long as I've been alive I've felt...alive."

Paul studied his hands. To him, each crack and callous was indisputable proof that he was, without mistake, alive outside of Thomas' conscience.

"It may be for the best that you don't think about it. After all, live or die, it's of no consequence following my own death. It isn't farewell I will bid to the world, it is the world who will grant me its valediction."

Thomas' arrogance did not upset Paul. It was a foil to his own sense of worthlessness. Paul felt a modicum of vicarious worth through Thomas' narcissism. Thomas was installed in his own mind as the paragon of excellence, of utter perfection, as the end-all, be-all of conscious existence. Paul felt that he was beneath all, a servant to all, a slave to his existence.

A recurring fantasy of Paul's was, at night while tucked under covers, imagining himself as the kind of man he would be if he were to surrender his soul to the void, adopting Thomas' in its place. If he were engaged to Bianca, permitted to look upon her naked body, granted license to caress her lustrous hair, to hold her, he would experience euphoria as he had never experienced before, and he would not squander it with another woman as Thomas was.

The driver finally finished liberating Thomas' purchase from its tethers, having been caught up in attempting to untie one particular knot which he had tied too tight.

"Hey, make yourself useful and help me bring this in," Thomas said. "Wait, hold on a second."

Thomas ran up to the front door and rapped on it.

Bianca answered dressed in her evening's finest, lips painted as crimson as Paul's blushing desire.

"Hello, Thomas."

Thomas was sure his absence had been driving Bianca mad, and her elation at the sight of him affirmed his feeling.

"Take a look, baby. I told you I'd be returning with a surprise."

"Thomas!"

"That couch is so uncomfortable to sleep on. There's no way I would let you sleep on it," he joked, slurring his words a bit. "This is a queen fit for a queen, with plenty of space for the both of us."

"Oh, Thomas."

Bianca descended from the front porch steps and embraced him. He held his darling and spoke softly so Paul could not overhear. It was not a secret told. It was a promise.

"I just want to be close with you during this time."

Paul stood by the wayside, disturbed at the scene. The Korean driver, too, visibly impatient, scowled at both men. Paul was aware of Thomas' infidelity, and his possession of this private fact was like an infection which, by refusing to treat it via its expression, spread to each corner of his conscience. The cross meant for Thomas to bear as penance for his sins was handed off to Paul who bore it without a grudge.

In his closed-eye fantasies, Paul imagined revealing the fact of Thomas' relationship with Asja to Bianca who would proceed to banish her unfaithful fiancé and grant Paul her hand in marriage. All would cheer for him and his courage as millions of spiraling strands of confetti stream over the crowd which would hoist Paul above their heads. The vine-ripened fruit would be harvested from the garden of his passions, a once barren lot that would then yield unending spoils; a fat peach tickling Paul's tongue as he samples the flesh before a juicy eruption, the firmness of young plump tomatoes surrendering to the pressure of Paul's groping hands and fingers, the sticky nectar trailing down the skin of the fruit waiting to be lapped up by Paul's eager tongue.

Paul envisioned himself succeeding with Bianca without incurring a debt of guilt. He thought to himself: what wars were not waged in desire's name, for the sake of forceful acquisition? What man has not dared to steal from his fellow man? What man has never once betrayed his closest friend? and from the womb of which of man's propensities do these selfish conceptions fall from? Is it envy which fathers man's vengeful designs?

Paul dreamt that he would, with no qualm whatsoever,

supplant Thomas and steal from him everything Thomas had accorded himself. Possession, for Paul, was a matter of entitlement. He believed Thomas was rightfully granted all he had, even Bianca despite his deception, for it was Thomas' ability to allow the intrigue to remain undiscovered that entitled Thomas to his engagement to Bianca. If he were not such an expert at deceit, he would, then, be entitled neither the pleasure of his weekly caprice nor the privileges of his engagement to Bianca.

Paul considered himself entitled to nothing and cheated out of everything. He was a poor, ugly Lilliputian of a man who smelled at all times of bitter anti-fungal powder and anti-itch creams. The last time he had laid his lips on a woman save for his mother was twelve years ago, and only five days after his first. He remained celibate, although this was not a feature of his character that he maintained by choice. His celibacy was the result of a careful attention to and preening of his social unease and slovenly appearance.

"Thank you for your help, Paul," Bianca said.

Both men lifted and maneuvered first the box spring and then the mattress into the bedroom.

"No problem," Paul said, panting.

His face was as flushed as the rosy shade of Bianca's lips, to which Paul offered a polite compliment.

"Oh, thank you, Paul."

"What's the occasion?"

Bianca clapped her hands together and glanced at Thomas adoringly.

"Thomas and I have plans."

"At Caneletto's," Thomas said.

He winked at Paul.

Paul's stomach churned in revolt against this revelation. Caneletto's was the restaurant at which Paul dined with his mother, whose receipt he would then relay to Thomas soon after penetrating another woman.

Bianca observed Paul's sudden lapse into sickness.

"Is everything alright?"

"Yes, yes," Paul replied. "It's just that that place—"

So close. The fires of Hell shone in Thomas' eyes as he scowled upon his thoughtless companion.

"I just can't think about it right now without getting sick."

"Why is that?" Bianca asked. "I thought you and Thomas dined there often."

"We do, but it's just that...well, the, um...Thomas always orders the garlic mashed potatoes with extra garlic."

Our hero Paul had saved face with an ambiguous admission, but, not content with a humble victory, began to run a victory lap around the course of his wit.

"I can't stand the smell of his breath after."

It was as good as true to Paul because his mother, Thomas' dinner-time double, would order the garlicky dish, except—

"Well, that's funny," Bianca said without a hint of humor. "His breath never smells of garlic when he comes home."

Thomas, standing a bit to Bianca's rear and just out of her peripherals, began pantomiming as though he were smacking his palm against his forehead at Paul's blunder.

"I mean—"

Paul cleared his throat.

"Excuse me. Well, uh...I've, you know, considering Thomas' choice in food, I've since started carrying mints."

He furnished a tin case of mints that he carried to treat his own awful breath, few of which he had ever shared with Thomas.

Bianca was pleased at this, although that is not to suggest that Paul's blunder had at all roused suspicion in any capacity. The mystery of Thomas' inoffensive breath was an insignificant anomaly to Bianca that was not worth investigating any further.

"Anyway, I am feeling a bit sick. I'll have to excuse myself. Or, I mean, you'll have to excuse me. My apologies."

"It's no problem at all, buddy. Let me walk you out."

Thomas commandeered Paul out of the front door with his hands tightly gripping his friend's shoulders.

"Goodbye, Paul," Bianca called.

"Goodbye, Bianca."

Paul was not able to turn his head to face Bianca as Thomas continued steering him forward.

Once outside, Thomas snapped at Paul in that amusing manner when one would prefer to shout but is absolutely bound to a negligible volume so that they are not overheard.

"What was that, Paul? Huh? What happened back there?"

"I...I–"

"The first line was enough. You did not need to go parading your charade. The mashes potatoes? The mints? Trust me, her suspicions were not running wild before you started running your mouth. It was a nice effort, Paul, but deceit does not suit you. Liberties like that could possibly endanger us both. Do you understand?"

Paul's eyes shined with moisture.

"I'm sorry. I didn't...I wasn't...I just tried to–"

"No, no. You know what? I overreacted. I'm sorry. Everything is fine. I have no reason to be upset. Just be more careful next time."

Paul simply nodded, bid his farewell and began walking home.

"Hey, do you have money for the cab home?" Thomas asked.

"No, that's quite alright. I can walk."

"I don't mind giving you fare for the cab."

"Well, if you insist."

Thomas fetched his wallet and handed Paul a large bill.

"That ought to do it, right?"

"Are you sure about this? A cab ride home doesn't cost this much."

"I'm giving him a good tip for all his help. Anyway, Bianca and I had better get going. Take care of yourself, Paul."

"Y-you, too."

Thomas returned inside and motioned to Bianca to suggest that they leave.

"Thomas, you're wearing my favorite cologne."

Thomas wrapped his arms around her and kissed her neck.

"You're wearing my favorite lipstick."

"Thomas, I'm sorry. Last night I–"

Thomas put a finger to her painted lips.

"Shh. Let's not get into that. Let's have a nice night out and enjoy ourselves."

Bianca smiled and kissed her love.

"Let me say goodbye to my dad real fast and then we'll leave."

When she returned, Thomas had risen from the couch and put his arm around his sweetheart as they made their way out.

The September evening was frigid owing to the wind that had been blowing for the better part of the evening. Bianca, despite her numerous woolen layers, was shivering. Thomas surrendered his overcoat to her and held her body near his to aid in keeping her warm.

Their downtown parking lot was one quarter of a mile away from the restaurant, and, on their way their, they soon lost patience for attempting to defy the wind's monopoly over their sense of hearing in order to be heard by the other.

In a manner more intimate than that of their earlier conversation, Bianca expressed to Thomas in various platitudes the depths of her love and her gratitude for his patience and attention to her needs, but to whom it was addressed was unknown for her words had been swept into a gale which muted her words and carried them away from Thomas.

CHAPTER SIX

Thomas decides on a date
for the wedding.

"You've been sleeping with her this whole time?"

"It's really none of your business."

"Unbelievable. You're trash."

"Believe it. I won't apologize."

Diners nearby were engrossed in the ensuing drama, their ears perked to catch the heightened pitch of the couple's yelling. The eyes of every patron followed the rise and fall of the pair's every exaggerated gesture.

"Trash, mate. That's what you are. A dog. A bloody dog."

"What a bunch of clowns," Thomas remarked.

Bianca giggled.

"They're obviously wasted."

The two friends burst out in laughter, their earnest charade finally cracked.

Said one to the other: "You shameless shit. Even I could have done much better. I can't wait until the boys back home get a load of this."

"I just wanted some American tail before we got back home, mate. Tell 'em all. They'll be jealous, aye? The lot of 'em. An' what 'av ya done since we've been 'ere, then, aye? Ya been 'avin' yaself a job tryin'a catch some tail, yeah? That's what."

"She was a dog, mate. A dog like you. A bloody dog. Ah'll bet when ya was shootin' off you was howlin' like a goddamn dog."

Thomas left a generous tip on the table and led Bianca by the hand out of the restaurant. They laughed over the rowdy boys as they walked about the shop-lit boulevards.

"So, Caneletto's is my new favorite restaurant," Bianca said. "I'm glad I've finally tried it."

"I've been trying to convince you to try it but you were never interested."

"Because you and Paul eat there all the time. I wanted to go somewhere neither of us had been to before, but now I don't care. The food was so good. Also, I'm a little drunk from the wine."

As they walked, Bianca would make intermittent turns in order to look at her's and Thomas' reflection in the shop windows. She appraised their appearance as a couple with the objective eye of an anonymous passer-by, inspecting them first from her peripheral and then with a head-on glance to better glean their collective appearance.

Bianca, a natural beauty in her own right, had bloomed beautifully after her escape from the clumsy blossom of adolescence. She kept the flower of her grace closely guarded and contained like a young rose whose petals remain curled inward; gorgeous to all who behold it but embarrassed to blossom outright. But her brilliant profile was offset by the shame of her supple body, of embarrassment over her womanhood.

In an honest encounter with her mirror image, she would find little she was happy with. Her reflection in the hungry eyes of other men moved her to regard her body and its feminine allure as a liability, as something that belonged not solely to her. Her femininity was an aspect of herself which she felt she did not have a right to, that it was something men had stolen from her and made to fit into a model of their design. After spying her reflection being guarded by the strong arms of the one she loved, she felt pure.

If purity was an idea denoting a total absence of qualities, then *Yes*, her mirrored double would proclaim to its twin, *I am pure*. All of the shame that had infiltrated her identity as a woman was dispelled by Thomas. He had robbed her of all insecurity, of any reason to feel ugly. Her radiance had collected grime through years of solitude and was cast in dust before it shined like sunlight through a diamond after being polished by Thomas' rejuvenating love.

Thomas noticed his darling continually turning towards the windows of the shops, believing that she was merely glancing upon the merchandise displayed in each shopfront. Each caught the other's eye in the reflection. Thomas stopped and turned to face a dimly backlit window which generously reflected their image without obfuscation. Bianca followed suit.

"Look how good we look together," Thomas stated.

Bianca's face, defiant of the sharp chill of the wind, was warmed by a love-stricken blush. She admired how synchronous she and Thomas had been in thought, how cognizant he was of that which she was privately devoting her thoughts to. She simply laughed, her humor sufficing as wholehearted agreement.

"I wouldn't look half as good standing next to any other woman as I look standing next to you."

He wrapped his arms around her as he spoke and rested his

chin on her shoulder to kiss her wind-blown cheek.

"I love you, Bianca."

Nature had yielded to man as it had not for woman— there was no howling of the wind, no absence of response to reduce his words to muteness, to whisk them away. The pale complexion of his lips was warmed by the burning blush of her face as their lips joined in silent whispers of insistent devotion.

Thomas played with the ring on Bianca's finger for a moment.

"You won't be wearing this old stone for much longer."

Her eyes pleaded for an explanation.

"Since Mary passed, I went ahead and rescheduled the date of our suspended wedding to coincide with the next sailing of Le Soléal. I want our marriage to be officiated on the same vessel your mother spent her last days on because I would like her to be present in spirit since she cannot be present in body."

Bianca's eyes began to water. The wet, cascading tails of tears stung as they trailed down her cheeks.

"Thomas, that's beautiful. I don't know what to say."

"Don't worry. When the time comes, all you'll need to say is 'I do.'"

CHAPTER SEVEN

Thomas envisions Ray's demise,
and instructs Paul in the ritual of seduction.

Thomas had gathered a small number of vials and individually wrapped capsules, then placed and allotted a number of each in small bags. With the prescriptions in hand, he passed through a corridor of cold white tile and walls yellowed with age to reach the elevator. Two doors of scratched and dented steel opened to present to Thomas a cramped enclosure lighted by two flashing bulbs that could not settle for either shining or dimming. Thomas, who often rode the elevator without company, played a game of saying his goodbyes to the world and those he knew as if each trip were his last.

"Goodbye, Paul, my squire. May you find another lord to serve. Goodbye, Asja, you who would be wise to be absent from my funeral. Goodbye, Bianca, the only woman I have ever truly loved. And farewell, Ray, who I shall visit soon enough inhabiting your own private estate in Hell."

The damaged elevator doors struggled to open, and when they did, Thomas clasped his hands and bowed ironically, thanking the skies for yet another safe journey. He traversed the yellowed labyrinthine halls of the corridor, ultimately entering a room in which a nurse was attending to the administration of an oxygen mask in order to manually ventilate a morbidly obese patient who suffered from challenging airway anatomy.

"Your order," Thomas announced.

"Hold this, please."

The nurse signed the printed order before tearing the contents from the bag. Thomas maintained the mask over the patient's face with overwhelming indifference while the nurse prepared a dose of suxamethonium chloride with which to inject the patient. The chemical was meant to tranquilize the patient in preparation for endotracheal intubation which would facilitate the ventilation of the patient's lungs.

Thomas observed the mouth-breathing patient, cringing at his condition. He observed the nurse administer the suxamethonium, imagining the patient struggling to draw its breath, gasping and choking with what little air it could take in.

What would it do as it died? he mused. Would it claw and grab at its neck as if seeking to free itself from a stranglehold? Perhaps it would seize the bed rail in a desperate fervor, its eyes bulging and convulsing in an attempt to surrender its final words that would not be able to escape from its obstructed airway.

Thomas had developed numerous ways to amuse himself in order to allay the boredom of his profession as a pharmacy technician, working hours which typically saw a lower volume of patients. He had taken to orating streams of absolute nonsense and gibberish when he was alone in the pharmacy. The luxury of noting the approach of a fellow technician in either the resonance of footsteps upon the metal stairs or the clatter and ring of the descending elevator allowed him the liberty of masturbation in his work space. He often touched himself to the thought of a female nurse entering the pharmacy and catching him in the act and then, following her initial shock, proceeding to provide her strict medical expertise to aid in his release. Among his work-time hobbies, fantasizing about the death of patients was one he was most fond of.

When the nurse was ready to intubate the patient, she bade Thomas leave. He did so silently. On his way out, he ensured that the nurse was engrossed in her duties before grabbing the signed order slip as well as the vial of suxamethonium and dropped it into his pocket. Her ignorance would be to blame for the loss of the vial.

He made his rounds delivering pharmacy orders to their respective recipients, none of whom had time or the desire to make small talk. He returned to the pharmacy to await further orders. In his minutes alone, he played with the vial of suxamethonium, spinning it on its side, rolling it back and forth across his desk between his hands. He kissed the vial and began singing in a demented impression of a child's voice:

"Ray, Ray, go away–won't live to see another day."

When Thomas had finished his shift he left to meet Paul at his home. Paul's haunts were a run-down and poorly managed apartment complex. The brick walls had been sprayed with countless painted murals and the streets within the complex were as pockmarked with potholes as a young man's pubescent face. The odor of sewer and grease hung heavy in the air and could be noticed more than a quarter of a mile away.

Why doesn't that greasy dwarf move somewhere else? Thomas thought. *Anywhere else, for Christ's sake.*

Thomas entered the complex and passed three shifty characters who dressed alike in black sweaters and torn denim jeans who silenced themselves as Thomas passed by.

Motherfuckers, Thomas said under his breath. *They're talking about me. Come on, you lowlifes, let's see you try something.*

He gripped the hilt of his pocket knife, a tool he regularly kept on his person. Thomas had always imagined what it must feel like to take a man's life, having ultimate power and absolute authority over another. The killer alone decided how those weaker than him would perish and what degree of pain they must suffer before their soul is split from their either carefully tortured or hastily dispatched corpse.

His gruesome fantasies were not satisfied following a hypothetical murder. He imagined the circumstances regarding how he would remain undetected and how he would elude the law. The most preoccupying ordeal was picturing the disposal of the corpse, the artistic cuts across limbs like strokes of a brush on canvas, the severed appendages, the purposeful gushing of blood, those final strained gasps of the victim struggling to catch one last full dying breath. Thomas believed that murder was an artistry few men possessed the courage to pursue serially. Even fewer were concerned with the aesthetics, the poesy of calculated killing and an artful disposal or treatment of the body.

He often hypothesized about how he would utilize the bodies; as upholstery, like Ed Gein; as sex slaves, like David Parker Ray; would he dine on their flesh? No. Thomas was content to picture each body expertly cut into dozens, hundreds, thousands of pieces for him to litter about the city like countless pieces of a jigsaw puzzle strewn about the corners and crevices of one's home. Some leave notes to taunt their pursuers. Thomas would leave slabs of his victims' flesh still attached to the subcutaneous fat.

He imagined the impromptu murder of the three hoodlums and being forced to avoid capture by the police. An exhilarating chase, a city-wide search, a media scandal would all ensue, but the juvenility and dimwittedness of homicide did not titillate him like his pleasurable fantasies of serial murder, and what a pleasure it seemed not only to take a life, but to torture a man to the utmost of their physical and mental threshold for pain. If only, Thomas wished, he was certain of his capability to avoid being found out, he would....

"Cowards," Thomas muttered when he had passed through a corridor out of sight of the shady men. "In any case, if Paul has made it three years here without being mugged or attacked, I suppose I'm okay."

Thomas amused himself by imagining Paul's neighbors waiting outside of his door every morning so they could rob him on the spot, that it was routine for that scared little worm of a man to be cornered and stolen from. Thomas knew that Paul would be quick to surrender his money rather than trying to talk the men down or defending himself.

Thomas turned the corner and followed a dark unlit corridor to its end. He rapped on Paul's door.

"Hey there, Thomas."

"Good afternoon, Paul. How are you?"

"I'm doing alright. I was...well, I was just cleaning before you got here."

Thomas took a look at Paul's kitchen. It was a cramped space only a short distance from the apartment door. One could not completely open the oven door before it would hit the cabinets across from it, and it appeared as though it had not been cleaned since Paul moved in years ago. The countertops, its tiles yellowed and surrounded by heavy grout, were littered with kitchen utensils that were spotted with sauce and weeks-old food that had dried and hardened on the metal. Thomas walked to the fridge to grab a bottle of water and watched as a cockroach scurried away from him, running under the fridge to hide.

"Jesus, Paul, you really need to call an exterminator or buy some traps or something," Thomas said. "It's disgusting how you are fine with living in this filth."

"I...I know. I talked to the superintendent about it. He's supposed to handle things like this but he refuses. I've been asking for weeks."

"Then you need to be the one to do something about it, don't you think? It has gotten way out of hand. You can't tell me that you're comfortable living like this."

"I'm...you know...I mean, nobody wants to live like this. If dreams did come true, and I know they don't, I would be living in a mansion with a garden out front with cactuses and azalea and...."

"Cacti," Thomas said.

"What?"

"It's 'cacti,' not 'cactuses.'"

"Oh. Well, I'd have a *cacti*," Paul said, stressing the word he had used incorrectly.

"Cacti is plural. You would have cacti."

Thomas noticed Paul's jawbone clench, presumably in frustration.

"I meant to say 'cacti', not 'a cacti'. I just–"

"Easy, easy," Thomas said, noticing his friend's pallor flush violently.

"W-well, if I...if you'd let me...if you weren't always correcting–"

"Alright, Paul," Thomas said, chuckling. "Go on."

"I would have cacti," Paul almost yelled.

Thomas nearly burst out laughing at his friend's mounting impatience.

"And I'd have a hedge maze. I would have servants and we would all drink wine and eat steak every day. I would have an observato—"

Thomas laughed at his friend's overexcitement.

"You're getting carried away now."

"I'm just trying to prove to you that it wasn't my dream to live here."

Paul's expression, responding to Thomas' teasing and his own self-pity, and comically changing each moment, was uncertain of whether to exhibit his frustration or his sorrow.

Thomas, still contending with the impulse to laugh out loud at his friend, said, "You haven't done anything to try and better yourself, though. You need to understand that dreams do not realize themselves."

"I guess you're right."

Paul took a seat on his old baggy couch.

"You either do what it takes at the end of the day or you don't, but you should know this. Anyway, I didn't come here only to upset you."

Paul wished to respond to Thomas with sarcasm but he opted for silence.

"So what did you come here for?" Paul asked.

Realizing his question may have sounded rude, he apologized and corrected himself.

"I just wanted to talk. This new stage of my life has been pretty strenuous. I feel like Bianca's father is turning her against me."

Thomas took a seat in Paul's tattered leather recliner and ran his hand through his hair.

"I try so hard to get along with this miserable old bag of bones but it's not possible. Bianca's an only child so she is his little princess. He acts like I'm stealing her away even though most of the time she's in his dark cloister of a room tending to his every need. The man is an infant nearly aged to death. He calls out, 'Bianca, Bianca,' every time her and I try to spend quality time with each other. I swear he's going to drive us apart, and he would die happy knowing he accomplished as much."

"What a terrible situation," Paul said. "How long is he, um, you know...how long does he maybe have left?"

"Hopefully not much longer."

"Well, don't think about it like that."

"That's exactly how you were thinking about it," Thomas shouted at Paul. "You asked how much longer he'll be alive. You were essentially asking me when he will be dead and thus when he can stop creating this mess."

"I...I guess I was."

"You need to think before you speak. You didn't want to take responsibility for thinking in a way that isn't very empathetic so you express yourself vaguely and transplant the idea into my head."

"I-I'm sorry," Paul stammered.

"It's fine. I'm just irritable lately. This whole ordeal has had me on edge. To top it all off, the amount of money we have spent tending to Ray has been more exorbitant than Bianca and I expected. I've been working additional shifts at the hospital to pay for everything, and Bianca stays at home all day tending to her father so she is exhausted before I even get home."

"Is there anything I could do to help?"

"Hell, I'd hate to ask you for help, buddy."

"I wouldn't mind helping out. I feel bad about what's happening. I can tell it has been tough for you. Just let me know if you need anything."

"Well...."

He hesitated for a moment—he had lied about working extra shifts at the hospital as well as the mounting expenses required to care for Ray. If Thomas were honest with Paul, he would have told him that, while it could not be denied that taking care of Ray was difficult, it was not quite as financially taxing as he made it out to be.

"Would it be too much to ask you for $250?"

"Um...."

Thomas tried to appear empathetic. He knew he already had Paul hooked–it was already as good as agreed upon.

"You know what? Forget it. Don't worry about it. I'm fine."

"No, Thomas. I insist."

"Paul, no. I'm sorry I asked. We're fine, really."

"No, really, it's okay. Here, look at this."

Thomas noticed spots of dust and dirt that were pressed into Paul's clothes from sitting on the old couch after he stood up. Paul grabbed a chair that had had its leather upholstery torn off after years of use and placed it on the linoleum floor in the kitchen. Standing atop the chair, he grabbed ahold of a ceramic vase painted with an oriental floral design. He stepped down from the chair and walked towards Thomas and set the vase on the coffee table adjacent to the recliner on which Thomas was seated.

Thomas seemed confused as he looked at the vase.

Paul took notice of his friend's expression.

"Watch."

He turned the vase upside down, ejecting a thick wad of dollar bills bound together by a rubber band.

"Jesus, Paul. Where the hell did you get all of this money?"

"I inherited it from my father after he passed away. It's not enough for the mansion of my dreams but it's something."

"You could move out of this rat trap, though, Paul–move somewhere decent."

"Could we maybe talk about that another time? I have my reasons. Anyway, here you go."

Paul unfastened the bills and handed Thomas a number of notes totaling $250.

"Wow, Paul. Thank you so much. I know I may not show it

but I appreciate our friendship, pal."

"Likewise, friend."

Paul was beaming; so glad to have been able to perform such an important service for his friend.

"Really, though, what do you have here? Thousands? Why do you keep all of this cash here? Deposit it. Go lease a home, rent a property elsewhere. Get out of this trash heap, Paul."

"Thomas, could I be honest with you?"

"Sure."

"The way I see it, what good is a nice home if I'm living alone? Don't you buy a house when you are prepared to share it? I'm lonely here. A more expensive property wouldn't help me feel any less lonely. If anything, I would have more open space to be lonely in. I wouldn't have many furnishings to put inside and it would look so empty."

"If you ever met a woman, you could not take her back here. You would meet women and take them home to a place you care enough to keep clean, show them a nice time, show them you know how to take care of yourself; that you're successful, clean, organized and established."

"I'm not good at meeting women, though. I can't talk to them beyond a friendly 'Hello.' I have no idea what else to say after that."

"You just lack confidence. You need to work on that first and foremost. A woman can sense a lack of confidence like sharks sense blood in the water."

"How do I work on changing that?"

"Here, how about this: let's you and I go to a bar tonight. You can hang back and observe my style. We can act as though we're not familiar so you don't feel self-conscious or uncomfortable about not joining in. Just relax and listen if you'd like. Eventually, though, we're going to need to put you in the shit. That's the ideal learning environment. The more you throw yourself into that dynamic the more comfortable you'll be creating it."

"I guess," Paul said with his signature stammer.

"Great, it's a plan, then. Our first order of business, though, is returning to my house so I can give this money to Bianca."

"Okay, that's fine. I'm ready when you are."

"Alright, let's get on our way, then."

He patted Paul on the back.

"Thanks again for doing me such a huge favor, pal."

"Don't mention it. Oh, just one thing."

"What is it?"

"Please don't tell Bianca I gave the money to you. You can tell her it's from working extra hours or you can tell her you got a bonus, or something."

Thomas had not intended to tell Bianca that the money was from Paul. He understood Paul well enough to know that he would not ever mention the loan to Bianca or ever ask for repayment, thus Thomas would not need to pay him back. If he were to tell Bianca the money was from Paul, she would pester Thomas until Paul was recompensed.

"Why is that?" Thomas asked for the sake of posterity. "She would think the world of you. Not to say she doesn't already think you're a great guy."

Thomas had stretched the truth–he and Bianca frequently made fun of Paul when he was not around. Bianca did not think him an unfavorable man but she did not think highly of him.

"Well, honestly, now you know I have all this money and I know you're judging me for staying where I am and not moving somewhere else, and I don't want to feel that pressure from both of you."

"I understand. This will be our secret," Thomas said as he placed his hand atop Paul's shoulder.

"Thanks."

"Don't mention it."

When they made it to Ray's, Thomas told Paul to wait outside.

"The old man wouldn't be very keen on having a guest in the home. He's hardly keen on having me in the house. Besides, who knows what kind of sickness is swimming around in there."

"That's fine. I'll wait here."

"Okay. I'll try and make it quick. I'm going to give Bianca this money, let her know what we're up to and I'll be right back. Hold tight."

Paul nodded, clasped his hands behind his back and began to walk about the front yard.

Thomas entered the home quietly and, being confident that Bianca would be with her father, sneaked into their bedroom. He grabbed one of his suitcases from the bedroom closet and undid the zipper on the front pocket, removing a small leather satchel. He transferred the money Paul had loaned him from his wallet into the bag and returned it to the front pocket of the suitcase.

Paul walked among the fallen leaves in the yard and turned his head to look toward the door as it sounded as though it had opened. He shook his head in confusion and continued pacing.

Inside the home, Thomas had crept back to the front door and opened it quietly so he could shut it and act as though he had just arrived. He called out for Bianca.

"Hey, babe," Thomas said, meeting her halfway up the stairs and wrapping her in his arms.

"Hey."

"How are things?"

"Oh, you know. He's not getting any better."

"Well, yeah. I know."

Thomas cringed.

"Oh, babe, would you mind if Paul and I went out for

drinks?"

"Why?"

"Well, Paul sort of broke down earlier and told me how lonely he is. I told him he needs to get out and meet a nice girl. He told me he has no idea how to talk to them. He greets them but anything beyond that to him is mysticism. I told him I would take him out and, you know, be his wingman–try and ease him into talking to a woman, and, you know, be a buffer between him and the woman because, left alone, he would mess it up."

"So you're taking him out to go hit on women?"

"Well, yeah."

"So you're going to spend the rest of your night with your friend hitting on other women while I stay at home? That's great."

"Okay, okay. You need to calm down."

"No, I'm calm. You go ahead and talk to other women at the bar. Why don't you fuck one of 'em, too? You may as well because you never fuck me."

Thomas winced.

"I am not going to be hitting on them, Bianca. Jesus. I'm doing this for Paul. I will strike up a friendly conversation, introduce my friend, and talk up his good qualities. If he starts slipping or feeling too pressured and withdrawn, I'll be there to play interference so the conversation doesn't die and leave him feeling awkward and hopeless."

"You're going to talk up his good qualities? What are those, exactly? Talk to me like I'm one of these other girls."

She could not stand the thought of Thomas flirting with another woman, even if it were to thereby draw attention to Paul. To think of Thomas being charming to other women–and what if they were attracted to him, if he could not refuse their advances?–was too painful for her to imagine.

"Look, if we have to lie to a few women about him having

qualities he doesn't actually have, what harm is that?" Thomas asked. "He needs a few practice runs before he goes off to the races on his own. Maybe he can play up on some qualities he does not possess, lie down with a woman or two and get the hell out of this hole he's in. I'm positive he's a virgin. When I ask him about it he shuts down and won't make eye contact with me, although he says he isn't. I don't know about you girls, but us boys die the first time we sleep with a woman. Our essence up to that point is reincarnated and we are given new life. The womb is a nexus of creation and grants the gift of life to more than a gestating embryo. It turns a boy into a man, gives him purpose and drive."

"Stop," Bianca said. "Just go. I don't want to see you, anyway."

"No need to be jealous. I promise I'll be good. I will watch Ray all day tomorrow and then you can go out for the night."

"Fine, okay. It's alright. I don't want to talk about it anymore. You can go."

"Thanks, babe. You're the best."

Thomas kissed her on the cheek.

Bianca turned around, shook her head and walked back upstairs. Thomas returned to the front door and exited the house, finding Paul in close study of a cracked, fallen leaf he was holding in front of his face.

"What is it saying?" Thomas, who was, until then, undetected by Paul, asked.

Paul jumped in surprise and turned around to face Thomas. He began laughing after the initial shock subsided.

"I didn't hear you come out."

Thomas laughed at his friend.

"What the hell were you doing?"

"Well, there wasn't much to do around here while I waited for you," Paul said with a smile.

"My apologies, sir," Thomas said with an ironic bow. "I'm here now so let's be on our way."

The two arrived at The Velvet Lounge later in the evening. It was a favorite of Asja's when she and Thomas were dating, but Paul had never been. Upon entering, Paul was amazed at the ambience and decor. The walls were lined with dark velvet and oil candles hung from the walls, basking the lounge in an intimate light. The lounge's choice in portraiture was strange. In one, a pale woman with feathered black hair and heavy green blush adorned in a zebra print leotard poses atop a tiger. In another, a black and white portrait features a woman with black flat bangs and shoulder-length hair in what looks like an open Roman temple, and she is done up in a flowing white dress spattered in dark handprints that seem to have been imprinted by bloody hands. Her right arm holds a knife and the bodies of three men clutching at their wounds are strewn about the temple. There was a sense of violence at play in the sexual ambience of the lounge that unnerved Paul, but he voiced no concern.

"I'm going to order you the strongest drink they've got," Thomas said. "You need to be comfortable and loose before we get things going."

Paul drummed his fingers on the table.

"What is their strongest drink?"

"It's the Velvet Curtain Call but everyone calls it a Curtain Call," Thomas explained. "No artist worthy of a curtain call bows before a curtain of any other material."

Paul let escape a light laugh.

"Why do they call it that? That's a strange name for their strongest drink."

"They call it that because it's the curtain call. It's the end. That's it for you, buddy. Take your drunken bow and stagger off the stage. You're done–finished."

"Are you sure about this?"

Paul was visibly worried.

"Yes. This is exactly why you need this. If you could see yourself you would notice how tense you are. Women will pick up on that. Remember one thing: don't seem tortured about not being able to find the words to say to a woman. I'll handle most of the talking and, as we're socializing and getting to know these girls, act confident even if you have nothing to say. It's better to act above the conversation, like your mind is on other things, than it is to act scared and worried because you don't know what to say. Women like a challenge and if there's something about you they can't quite put their finger on, they'll feel compelled to get to know you, to understand you. If you act self-conscious, these women won't want to waste their time. Got all that?"

Paul nodded and continued drumming on the table.

Thomas grabbed his hands.

"You're going to need to learn how to watch that. I'll go order the drinks. I'll be right back."

Unbeknownst to Thomas, Paul had concealed the extent of his fright. He seemed outwardly nervous, yes, but, in actuality, he was terrified. He pictured the scenario before he was forced into it–Thomas would pull two woman to their booth, Paul seated closest to the outside next to a woman with the other woman seated near Thomas. The conversation would flourish with Thomas engaging the entire group, but, after he had guided the conversation until everyone was relaxed and comfortable, they would diverge into two smaller groups with Thomas paying exclusive attention to the woman nearest him, leaving Paul alone with the other woman. The conversation would be a bust. Paul would fumble for the right words, eventually surrendering and resigning himself and his partner to silence.

Thomas returned with the drinks.

"Alright, here we go. Bottoms up. We need to get you in a

good spot before we get the ball rolling."

The drink was poured into a large cocktail glass and tinted a dark blue to match the lounge's velvet wallpaper. It tasted especially sweet to Paul.

"What is this?" Paul asked, seeming suddenly flustered.

"What do you mean?"

"This drink is so sweet. Is this, like, some placebo where after I drink it I'll feel drunk and we'll talk to these girls and after we hit it off you'll say, 'Wow, Paul, it was in you all along,' and you'll tell me you ordered me a virgin drink?"

Thomas laughed.

"You're going to wish it was. That's got about five shots of liquor in it, pal. You're just tasting the liqueurs."

"Five shots?" Paul asked. "I'm in for it now."

Paul shut his eyes and sipped his drink until he filled his mouth with the saccharine cocktail. Thomas was amused as he watched his friend begin to drink in a haste before he could think twice. Paul's throat bulged as he swallowed mouthfuls of his drink. He had finished a little less than half when Thomas had only consumed about a quarter of his–an impressive feat for Paul, whose drink was much larger than Thomas'.

"You're doing great, Paul. I'm proud of you. Keep going. Feel it, don't fight it. Just relax and embrace this feeling as it comes."

Paul had never developed an appetite for alcohol, only indulging in a solitary glass of cheap wine on particular occasions. There was no room for conversation between Paul gulping his cocktail. He continued to make progress on his drink, seeming as though he were straining himself to finish, like he was in competition with everyone in the room. He made faces identical to a man straining to lift as much weight as his strength would let him.

Thomas excused himself to order another round once Paul

had nearly finished his first drink.

"This time I'll order you a weaker drink you can tend to for a while while we socialize. Get ready. I'll be back with some ladies."

Paul watched Thomas lean over the counter and speak to the bartender as though they were old friends. Thomas' back was turned to Paul, but he watched the bartender as he would smile and laugh. Paul envied how charming Thomas was to strangers. He envisioned both ladies he would bring to the table both being irresistibly drawn to Thomas and neglecting him.

Thomas then sat next to two women and immediately charmed them into a state of laughter.

Poor Bianca, Paul thought.

Paul believed Thomas could have any woman he wanted. He did not need Paul here. He could go home with both of these women if he wanted, but–Paul needed to reassure himself of this–Thomas was doing this for his benefit. He noticed his friend pointing him out, and the two woman did not laugh as he had expected them to. They spared no reaction. He wondered what Thomas could have told them to have elicited such a sensational non-reaction.

Paul did not doubt that Thomas was accounting for each of Paul's shortcomings as a man, that Thomas had brought him to serve as a contrast to his own strengths over Paul's. His failures would highlight Thomas' success in life.

The group stood up and made their way over to Paul's table. He began bouncing his right leg as fast as he could and clenched his teeth until they ached. Thomas has already ruined it, Paul thought.

There's no hope for me. He only used me as a pawn to draw attention to him.

"Paul," Thomas said when he reached the table. "This is Tabitha."

She extended a hand adorned with a number of rings and metal circlets to shake Paul's.

"N-nice to meet you, Tabitha," Paul said, struggling to muster a smile.

"And this lovely lady is Gabby."

She stood next to Thomas and made no effort to approach Paul, only nodding at him, smiling. He tried to maintain his forced smile and nodded back. Thomas gestured to Paul to take a seat and moved to the middle of the booth with Thomas seated next to him. Thomas waved Gabby over to sit next to him, leaving Tabitha to sit with Paul. Paul immediately judged her, who was not as fetching as her friend, to be too high-class for someone like him. She was outfitted in so many accessories that Paul guessed that she expected her potential suitors to be wealthy, not knowing her jewelry was mostly plastic and made to look but not feel authentic. Perhaps he would be better suited to Gabby who seemed more modest, dressed in a simple black dress with small ruby studs in her ears, but Thomas always won out over Paul.

Thomas leaned over and whispered to his friend.

"You have cancer."

"What?"

"I told them that you have cancer."

"Wait...."

"I'm sorry to hear about your condition," Gabby said in an accent he could not place.

"Yeah, it's awful. He just found out today," Thomas said. "This was his idea to come out, actually. I expected him to want to go home and brood over it. You know, that's probably what I would have done if I were him, but he's handling it very well. He told me, 'You know, I could use this as an excuse to give up now, to let the cancer win, but I won't go out like that. I'm going to live my life before my time so that when people look back on my life they can say I lived it with integrity, that I didn't give up for anything.'"

"Wow," Tabitha said. "You're very brave. I respect that."

Paul smiled with unease and all he could think to offer were his thanks.

"My father developed cancer when I was still just a little girl, back when we were still living in Bosnia," Gabby said. "I was eight years-old and he moved us all here to America for his treatment. My parents didn't enroll me in school until he had become bedridden and, before that time, my parents took me all over the country. We went to Disneyland, all sorts of museums and amusement parks, we took a helicopter up to the Grand Canyon; we travelled to so many places. My father was always so busy with work in our country and would come home before bedtime and then wake up before I had to go to school. He had worked very hard to provide for us because he had grown up very poor, and mother explained to me years later that he told her that he did not want me to remember the times he wasn't there but the times that he was. I lost my father when I was ten years-old but I will always remember him as a great man."

"That's really touching," Thomas said. "Your father was a strong man."

"Yes, he was."

"You know, so many people use any obstacle that gets in their way as an excuse to give up," Thomas said. "That only demonstrates how weak they are as men. My friend Paul here isn't like that. The way he has handled it so far, the things he has said to me demonstrates a strength that I don't even think I could have when faced with the same adversity."

Paul jumped when he felt an arresting sensation around his groin. He looked down and saw Tabitha grabbing his thigh and then looked up to see her gazing at him with glazed-over bedroom eyes.

"Stay strong," she said. "You'll make it through this."

Something in Paul had gone missing, a mechanism of self-consciousness that had been erased. It was as though his being had disintegrated. In its place was the essence of a man who did not recognize inhibition. He could no longer control his actions and watched without fear as his hand ventured toward Tabitha's. He observed his fingers sprawl out over hers, taking them in among his own. Tabitha's expression was the catalyst to a release of chemicals leading him unto the realization of a feeling he had never felt before. Was this love? The world and its possibilities had at that moment opened to Paul. He had taken Tabitha's hand and was guided through a portal into paradise. He glanced over at Thomas, who was wise to what he had done. He raised his eyebrows to Thomas as if to say, *Can you believe this*?

Thomas winked at him knowingly as though, through his gesture, he meant to reply, *See? This is what life is all about. Now you understand*.

Paul's future manifested before him in those lucid moments. He envisioned his future home, imagined leading Tabitha, who was eager for Paul to possess her, into his bedroom which would be decorated with expensive furniture, paintings and sculptures. Paul now held the highest-hanging fruit that he had ventured to pick after doubting his capability for so many years. He had made contact with a woman and was defibrillated by the convulsive shock of her beauty.

"It will be tough but I know I will make it," Paul heard himself say.

His words sounded as though they echoed from an orifice that was not his. He looked deep into Tabitha's eyes as she held his gaze.

Has it always been this easy? Paul wondered.

He felt uncontrollably happy, inconsolably celebratory, and he found it humorous that he had always been fearful of the process of seeking a mate. He felt that he had discovered how simple it was.

Tabitha had been the first to break eye contact. Paul sat there gazing upon her like she were a trophy he had won. When she looked away from Paul, she looked at his lap with rosy cheeks and sounded a shy laugh before she took her hand back. It had not seemed a discouraging sign to Paul as it would have if he were sober. He recognized her gesture as shyness and felt compelled to continue playing this romantic game.

He looked over at Thomas again who had his legs crossed, his left over his right, to shut out everyone but Gabby. He had his arm around her, a cue that made Paul consider how he could convince Tabitha to permit such a gesture. Thomas caught Paul observing him in his peripherals and turned slightly to acknowledge him and give him a thumbs-up with the hand that was draped around Gabby's neck.

Paul did not need to hunt for the words to say. He was able to channel appropriate talking points he had overhead in everyday conversation. He heard Thomas whisper to Gabby what he then decided to say to Tabitha.

"So...that's enough about me," Paul said, still not able to completely elude his stutter, although it did nothing to assuage his confidence. "What about you?"

"What do I do, you mean?" Tabitha asked.

Paul nodded.

"I'm a student. I'm working on getting my degree so I can become an RN."

"An RN?"

"Registered nurse."

"Wow," Paul replied, acting knowledgeable of the profession. "I heard...I...I heard that getting, you know, getting... going through medical school and all that is very difficult."

"It is, yes. It's rare that I am able to come out like this."

"Well, it's nice that you were able to. I enjoy talking to you."

The night proceeded with the pairs devoting their attention to one another, both groups so immersed in their partner that neither Paul nor Thomas had looked over to monitor the other's progress. Thomas had not noticed Paul initiating physical contact with Tabitha and Paul did not notice the sexual tension between Thomas and Gabby who were pawing at each other under the table. Thomas and Gabby whispered into each other's ear with Thomas, now and again, pronouncing the end of his secrets with his tongue softly caressing her ear lobe.

When the two had worked each other into over-excitement, Gabby stood up from her seat with her hand clasped in Thomas'.

He turned to Paul, his face betraying his concern.

"She's feeling sick. I think she had too much to drink. I'm going to make sure she's alright. I'll be right back."

Paul nodded and said nothing. He was in a haze of ecstasy, feeling as though he were dreaming, and he was overjoyed to recognize that his intoxication made the situation no less real.

Paul kept the conversation moving forward with moderate ease and felt himself slip away the more he drank. He was proud of his metamorphosis, and wished to remain this way for the rest of his days. His most miserable years were overshadowed by this crowning achievement of his. He had, on this unconquerable evening, been making significant contact with a woman, resisting the uncontrollable urge to kiss Tabitha. He had already succeeded in placing his arm around her and she was not repulsed by his action. Now, how was he to go about kissing Tabitha, kissing the second woman he would have ever kissed, his first kiss in over a decade?

"Tabitha."

She looked up from her hands which were occupied with fidgeting with the swizzle stick that came in her drink. She looked at Paul curiously, as though she had been waiting for him to say the right thing, for him to cross the verbal boundary into the physical.

"I've really enjoyed talking to you tonight," Paul continued.

His heart began racing as he fabricated his next statement in his head. For a moment, he had considered abandoning his plan to express himself, but he had already been given the ripened fruit. Why would he give up before tasting it?

"You're beautiful," Paul said, stunning himself. He sat in awe of what he had just accomplished. Never before had he been so bold.

"Thank you. You're handsome as well," Tabitha replied.

They watched each other for a few moments, each wondering who would make the move. Paul had gained clearance for the approach but he had stalled. Tabitha once again laughed in her shy manner, and it was this cue that convinced Paul to disregard his idle chatter and deny his mental faculties so his body alone could rule.

He leaned forward and bridged the short distance between the two, coming ever closer until finally came unparalleled bliss. There was rapture in Tabitha's lips which had delivered him from every self-imposed hindrance. He felt the uglier parts of himself being whittled away until he was refined and polished into a brilliant Adonis. Tabitha's hands began traveling across Paul's body. Paul's hands followed suit along Tabitha's body until he had become acquainted for the first time to the unbridled pleasure of orgasm facilitated by a partner.

Paul broke contact and leaned over the table. It seemed to Tabitha as though he would wretch any second.

"What's wrong?"

"Maybe too much...I think I had more to drink than I should have," Paul answered.

"Here," Tabitha said as she began sliding out of the booth.

"You should go to the bathroom."

Paul nodded and walked to the lavatory with his hands clenching his stomach. Once he stepped inside he made his way to a stall, shut the door and sat on the toilet fully clothed. He sighed in relief and began laughing.

What a maddening sensation.

The area near his pubic bone just above his groin felt like it was on fire and his penis was clenched incredibly tight as he released. Every orgasm produced by his own hand could not at all parallel the one he had at Tabitha's hands, and to compare the intensity of the two would be to compare the heat of the sun with that of a flame. He was still throbbing.

Paul undressed and cleaned the fluid that had soiled his underwear and, before he exited, lined the wet marks with toilet paper. When he stepped out of the bathroom, he discovered that Thomas and Gabby had returned. Gabby's hair was a bit disheveled. What seemed peculiar to Paul was Thomas' incessant smiling and easy laughter, and why Gabby was in such high spirits. Did she not, just moments ago, Paul thought, finish vomiting?

"Is everything alright?" Paul asked as he took his seat.

"Yes, of course," Thomas replied. "Is everything alright with you?"

"I'm fine now. I just had an episode.

Paul turned to Gabby.

"You guys, um, you seem happy for being sick just a moment ago."

Thomas, who was on the verge of laughter, raised an eyebrow and looked at Gabby who was combating laughter as well. The couple finally surrendered to their encroaching laughter together.

"Well, I had to throw up. I feel so much better now that it's all out."

"Oh, it all came out, alright," Thomas said. "And it went everywhere."

The pair burst into laughter once again.

Paul was confused as to what was so humorous regarding Gabby's sickness.

"It's getting late. I think we had better head back. I don't know about the rest of you but I've got quite the busy day tomorrow," Thomas said.

"Yeah, we'd best get going, too," said Tabitha.

The group all stood up from the booth and made toward the exit. Tabitha snaked her arms around Paul's left arm and leaned into him.

"I had a nice time tonight."

"I did, too, Tabitha."

Tabitha separated from Paul and said, "I want you to have this."

She handed him a napkin with her telephone number scrawled next to a handwritten heart.

"Great. Thanks. I'll be sure to...I'll call you sometime."

The two pairs embraced and exchanged intimate farewells before shaking hands and saying goodbye to the other group. Thomas stood and watched as the two women walked away.

"Now that was something, wasn't it?" Thomas asked.

"Oh, my God, it was."

Thomas turned to Paul and eyed him in surprise.

"Oh, yeah? Did you hit it off with Tabitha?"

"Yeah. Look at this."

Paul furnished the napkin with Tabitha's name and number written into the patterned cloth.

"Yes! Yes! You did it."

Thomas wrapped his arms around Paul's waist and hoisted him into the air.

"That's my boy!"

Paul had never felt such happiness in his life. He felt like he had been lifted above the world, above every challenge, every hardship, every regret. It was all worth it. Life's mathematics, however challenging it had been up to that point, had equalled this magnificent sum.

"Look at you, motherfucker," Thomas said, his voice booming and crackling with laughter. "You're beaming."

Paul blushed and smiled through his embarrassment.

"How did things go with Gabby?"

"Oh, you know, things were going well until she got all sick."

Thomas wore an ironic expression as he explained to notice whether or not Paul saw through the ruse.

"That's too bad," Paul replied.

Thomas tried to bottle his laughter as he spoke.

"Yep. It's really too bad, not that it matters because, you know...."

Thomas flashed his engagement ring.

"Bianca."

Thomas began walking and Paul followed.

"Well, how do you feel?" Thomas asked. "You feel like a new man, don't you?"

"I do. I really do. I had no idea that I could feel like this. It's almost stupid. Everything happened like I had no control over it. I just watched as it all unfolded and, next thing I know, Tabitha and I were kissing."

Thomas pushed Paul.

"You kissed her?"

Paul smiled and nodded.

"You son of a bitch," Thomas shouted. "Oh, man, this is great. I'm proud of you, buddy. I did not expect so much from you. Even your stutter has disappeared. You really pulled through, pal. I hope you're proud of yourself."

"I am," Paul said through a shining smile.

He was surprised Thomas was acting in such a way, this cold and often critical friend of his. When Paul was with Thomas he often felt like he were stumbling through a dungeon laden with traps and pitfalls, searching carefully for a treasure that would win Thomas' approval, but Thomas usually reacted to Paul's efforts with impatience. At that moment he felt like he had discovered and drank from the Holy Grail.

"That alcohol works wonders," Thomas said.

"I guess it does."

"Well, here is our fork in the road. This is where we part ways."

Thomas extended his hand which Paul duly grabbed.

"You did a hell of a job tonight, Paul. Nice work."

"Thanks."

"Goodnight," Thomas said.

"Goodnight."

The night became memory's domain as Paul recollected everything he had said and done with Tabitha, reliving certain moments numerous times. This brought him great pleasure, but as he cataloged every happening he remembered how much he had drank, and his mind brought him back to Thomas' comment: *That alcohol works wonders.*

The night would not have played out at all like it had if it were not for the alcohol he had consumed, Paul realized. It had transfigured him into somebody else–someone brave, someone worth knowing, worth kissing. Alcohol made him somebody who was worthy of being loved. Tomorrow he would wake up sober, boring and anxious as always.

He could leave his entire life behind, forgetting everything, replacing every memory with that of this night. His true nature laid dormant up until this day, awakened by the intoxicating bitter nectar.

When he was near his neighborhood he stopped at a nearby grocer. He made his way to the liquor aisle—so many choices. Paul figured each liquor was like considering different paths leading to the same Eden, and so, to save himself the trouble of deliberation, he decided on a whiskey that had caught his eye. He made his purchase and continued home with his bounty in a paper bag, taking infrequent swigs from the bottle as he travelled. The taste was sharp and overwhelming and his chest burned with every swallow, making him feel as though the whiskey was rejuvenating him, reinvigorating his heart which he could feel beating harder with purpose the more he drank.

What a wonderful world, Paul thought, marveling to himself. *What a purely splendid place we've been given. Good evening, stars. I see you shining bright and, though you are beautiful, you cannot match the searing and explosive shine of my soul. Good evening, moon, and why are you not full tonight? Do you wane in fear of not equaling the full-bodied magnificent glow of the beauty I have found here on this earth?*

"I have discovered the triumph of life," Paul shouted to the angels.

A shocked passer-by appeared in Paul's peripheral. He laughed to himself and lowered his volume, whispering to those same angels, "I have been given wings. Watch me take flight and take my place among you."

He hummed a joyful tune and laughed to himself as he walked through the corridor to his apartment.

Once inside, he went into the kitchen, erupting in laughter after stumbling over the refuse that littered his kitchen counter. He fetched a water-spotted glass from the dishwasher and poured his whiskey into it, sipping it as he stumbled toward his couch. Paul took a long draw from his glass and set it down onto the coffee table.

"Tonight, all of this disappears. I am henceforth a new man. Goodbye to everything and a how-do-you-do to my new life. I will wake up in a mansion with Tabitha next to me and we will be married and totally naked."

His declaration was interrupted by a hiccough which then caused him exaggerated laughter.

"Goodbye, life. Goodbye to everybody and everything."

Paul switched on his bedroom light and collapsed on his mattress, falling asleep shortly thereafter.

Thomas climbed into bed, waking Bianca.

"How was it?" Bianca asked sheepishly.

Her tone implied suspicion.

"It was a smashing success," Thomas cried, his enthusiasm snapping Bianca out of her lethargy. "You should have seen Paul, the awkward little cretin. He was so unlike himself tonight. I bought him a stiff drink to get him feeling good and he ended up kissing this girl and getting her number."

"Paul did all that? Paul?"

"Yes, our dear, precious little trolll," Thomas said. "He's all grown up now. Just you watch. I have changed his life. Well, kissing a woman did the trick but it never would have happened if it weren't for me. He's going to clean his apartment, save his money, burst out of his shell and become a man."

"Good for him," Bianca said. "You're *such* a miracle worker."

She dragged the second syllable, pronouncing it with a mocking drawl, to emphasize the irony of her words.

"Yeah, I know it."

Thomas leaned over and kissed Bianca on the neck.

She chuckled.

"Stop. That tickles."

"I know you like it."

Thomas wrapped his hand around her throat and kissed her neck.

Bianca moaned. She reached her hand down into Thomas' briefs and started to toy around with him. Thomas continued kissing her neck and her face as Bianca pulled on his member trying to coax it into an erection, but she stopped when it would not respond.

"Whatever. You neglect me all day and night and then you can't even fuck me."

"I'm sorry, baby."

Thomas kissed her once more.

"I thought I didn't have much to drink but I guess I had one beer too many. I'll make it up to you."

Thomas' musk did not reflect how much he drank because he had taken care to mask it, so Bianca did not quite believe him.

"Goodnight," Bianca said.

"Goodnight," Thomas echoed.

He had tried to sound remorseful, afterward feeling that he had failed. He turned so he was facing away from Bianca and relived his encounter with Gabby until he fell asleep.

CHAPTER EIGHT

Thomas, having suffered in the somber house with
Bianca, enjoys the pleasure of solitude.

The next morning, Thomas awoke to the appetizing smell of breakfast being cooked. He stretched before he got out of bed and walked lazily into the kitchen where a plate of waffles and syrup, fruit, cottage cheese, orange juice, and coffee awaited him.

"Wow, this is great, honey," he said. "Thanks."

"No problem."

Bianca's tone betrayed the calm air of her words.

Thomas ignored the bait she had cast to lure him into asking her what was wrong and began eating. He finished his meal quickly. When he pardoned himself from the table to put his dishes in the sink, he kissed Bianca on the cheek.

"You're the best, baby."

At that instant, Bianca tore off her dishwashing gloves and threw them in the sink.

"You know what, Thomas? I'm sick of it."

"What? Where is this coming from?"

"I'm sick of it," Bianca repeated. "I'm sick of everything. I'm sick of you, of this house, of you leaving me here by myself. I'm sick of you not being able to have sex with me. I'm sick of my father dying in front of my eyes. I can't take it anymore. The worst part is that I am going through all of this alone. You told me you would help take care of things with me but you've done nothing but keep your distance. We're drifting apart and, honestly, I don't think we're going to make it through this."

"Don't say that. We're going to make it through this together."

"I mean it. As it stands now, I am not interested in continuing this relationship after my father passes. You've already demonstrated your lack of concern for me."

"Then why the hell would I stay here and put up with all of this bullshit if we're just going to split after?"

"Thomas, you don't put up with anything now in the first place. When things began getting difficult, you threw in the towel. This whole thing has been so easy for you and it's not just my father who is dying. This is killing me, too."

"Listen, I would not have volunteered for this if I didn't love you and if I did not believe our marriage to be a worthy incentive following this ordeal."

"That's just not true. This has not been an ordeal in any capacity for you, and you do nothing to show me that you care for me besides tell me that you do."

"This hasn't been an ordeal for me? Are you kidding me? How about your father doing his best to tear us apart, trying his absolute hardest to turn you against me? You sit in his dreary room all day and night, absorbing his hatred. Maybe you were resistant to it at first but, after hearing about how terrible I am all day every day, you've started to believe him."

"Well, if my fiancé who claims to love and care for me would relieve me from tending to my father all day I wouldn't be stuck in there and forced to listen to it."

"You don't have to be stuck, Bianca. The old man doesn't need for that much. You don't need to feel like you're some sort of captive in there waiting for me to free you, or like you're his jailer."

"I'm not going to neglect my father like you neglect me, Thomas. He is dying. I am his only child. I am all he has left in this world. He was doing fine until my mother died, and now his grief has made him ill. He wasn't always fatigued and he could walk just fine before my mother died. He could live. I'm going to be by his side until the very end, and I will not leave my father alone while he slowly slips away. He's all that I have left of my family and I will *not* neglect him. He needs me, Thomas, much more than you do."

She attended to her watering eyes before she continued.

"See, this is your problem: you're so goddamn selfish. You don't think about anyone else's side. You only consider how hard this has been for you, how hard it has been to hardly see me, to feel stifled and depressed in this house. What about me, Thomas? What about the endless hours I spend here without you, sitting next to my father as he sleeps, as he lies immobile until his hunger or bodily functions wake him so I can immediately tend to his needs? What about the fact that my fiancé cannot fuck me most of the time? What about *my* solitude, Thomas? *My* despair, *my* hell, *my* dying father, Thomas?"

"Listen to you yell. You should go look at the disgusting scowl on your face. Your father has turned you against me. Finally. Just what he always wanted. So this is it? This is the end? We're finished, is that it? Is that what you want, to be really and truly alone with no family left after Ray? No fiancé, no friends, no guidance, no help, just lonely days with nothing but your solitude to keep you company? What an empty life. What a miserable fucking story. Living like that, you won't be far behind your father, Bianca."

"Get out!" Bianca screamed. "Get out of here. You disgust me. We're finished. We should have been finished a long time ago. Take your clothes with you and find somewhere else to stay. I don't want you back here. I don't even want to think about you. You can come back in a week and pack up your things but for now you are not welcome in this house or my life."

"Fine. I'm sure your dad is awake and waiting to hear from you. Go ahead and tell him in full detail what happened, and be sure to include what a piece of trash I am. He would love to hear that. Who knows? Maybe he will be so happy he has torn us apart that all of this will add years to your father's life. He'll probably leap out of bed and jump for joy."

"Stop talking. Get out. I won't say it again. One more word and I'll call the police."

Thomas took some time gathering and packing his clothes, cursing Ray and Bianca all the while, and, once he had finished, he stormed out of the house with suitcase in hand, slamming the door behind him. He was so angry he wanted to explode in anger; yell as loud as he could, topple over everything he passed. He wanted to run back to the house and murder Bianca. After her disposal, he would see to the torture of Ray, exercising caution to not allow him to die from physical trauma before he had tormented the old man to his satisfaction. He would be surrounded, snipers and SWAT teams posted near the house, and he would lay waste to them all with a single 9mm handgun and manage to hijack an armored vehicle and cross over the Canadian border into freedom.

Though his violent fantasy was ridiculous and fantastical, it had helped to console him. Thomas could not die in his fantasies. He could escape from any struggle free of harm and was invulnerable and always triumphed over odds that neared impossibility.

He traveled downtown where he had designs to stay at an older hotel. After he had checked in and had a bellman deliver his luggage to his room, he set off to a nearby liquor store. Once inside, he purchased a bottle of dark spiced rum, ginger beer and angostura bitters. He returned to his hotel and found the bellman who had handled his luggage.

"Good afternoon," Thomas said.

"Good afternoon, sir."

His porter, as far as Thomas noticed, always kept his hands clasped in front of his midsection unless he reached out to grab ahold of something. He seemed pleased to see Thomas again.

"Could you do me a favor?" Thomas asked.

"Of course, sir. How may I help you?"

"Could you deliver this bag to room number 1251?"

Thomas handed the bellman a fifteen-dollar tip.

"My pleasure, sir."

Deciding to tour the boulevard, Thomas set off from the hotel property and made his way to the main street. The dirty luster of the boulevard at nighttime was not apparent during the day. With the droves of people on a drunken stroll about the boulevard absent and the scores of neon lights and signs turned off, downtown seemed remarkably empty. Only the employees of surrounding properties, construction workers, lawyers en route to their office, and the homeless populated the streets. There were a number of dirty locals loitering in the alleys that Thomas tried to steer clear of, but one could not resist shouting at Thomas despite their significant distance from one another.

"'Ey, man. 'Ey you, white boy."

Thomas looked over with a challenging glare that the man disregarded. He walked from out of his alley toward Thomas, lowering his volume as he approached, speaking without regard for those nearby.

"'Ey. Lookin' for that white lady?"

"White lady?"

The man looked at Thomas and smiled.

"Yeah? Is that you that was lookin' for her? That white lady?"

The stranger wiped his nose, sniffing as though his nose were running.

Thomas could not mistake the gesture.

He took a cautious glance of the encompassing area before handing the man a twenty. His solicitor shoved the money into his pocket and rummaged in another. The stranger pretended as though Thomas had given him a donation.

"Thank you so much. I appreciate it."

He extended his hand to shake Thomas'. Thomas took his hand and gripped the small bit of plastic from the man's hand and immediately pocketed the matter.

"God bless," the stranger said.

Since Thomas inadvertently came into a grip of cocaine he figured it best not to use alone. This decision preceded his inspiration to hire a prostitute, an affair that would offer little difficulty in this city. Prostitutes advertised in the back pages of the city's weekly paper, disguising the actual services they provided with thinly veiled euphemisms.

Thomas continued to tour the boulevard, although little was offered in the way of visual stimulation in the daytime. The daylight exposed the degradation of the poorer corners of the city, allowing one to glimpse into the lost and still losing wretches who fashioned their asylum from the city's refuse.

The city's destitutes littering the boulevard disgusted Thomas, they who were of no use to anybody, they from whom there was no sort of loss when they were to die. To him, the homeless were lower than insects, each a parasite. They depended on the benediction of those above them to survive. They were leeches latching on to anybody who was above them.

All throughout the day, Thomas did not spare a single thought to what had led to him seeking refuge in the city. He smiled and joked with those he dealt with. It would be the sad side of the city, vulnerable, and with its degradation highlighted by daylight that oppressed him, not his exile. After dining in a nearby casino, he decided to return to his hotel room.

Thomas approached the entrance to his hotel and greeted the familiar bellman. He waved at the porter who, after spotting Thomas, sprinted to the door to open it for him.

"I appreciate it," Thomas said. "You work too hard, you know that? They ought to give you a raise."

"Thank you for the kind words, sir. Enjoy the rest of your day."

Thomas entered the hotel. To his immediate right stood the Guest Services desk. He approached the attending coordinator.

"Excuse me."

"Good evening, sir. How may I assist you?"

"I'd like to speak with a manager."

"Just a moment, please. Let me see if one is available."

Moments later the manager emerged, followed by the coordinator.

"Good evening, sir."

The two men shook hands.

"That bellman out there," Thomas began. "The uh, ah, what's his name?"

"Which one?" the manager asked as he scanned the outside.

"That one: the Hispanic one who never stops smiling."

Thomas fingered the man in question.

"Oh, yeah," the manager said, smiling and nodding his head in acknowledgment. "That's Cervantes."

"I just want to let you know he's the best goddamn luggage

agent I've ever dealt with. I've stayed at numerous hotels all around the country, and none of them could compete with Cervantes. I wanted to let you know you have one the country's finest bellmen working for you."

"Well, thank you for letting me know. I'll be sure to tell him about it."

Thomas smiled and shook the manager's hand.

"Of course. Take care, now."

Thomas had lied, of course, or perhaps had merely stretched the truth, but is not dishonesty often praised, or, at the very least, excused, if done with charitable intentions? He could not discern what had prompted such a kind gesture. Thomas only knew he had felt liberated since being kicked out of Ray's home.

Passing a newsstand in the elevator lobby of the hotel, Thomas grabbed a copy of the city weekly, and once he arrived at his hotel room, he laid down and flipped to the back pages through the advertisements section that was devoted to massage parlors and prostitutes. He perused the ads for some time, appraising the physical assets of each prostitute pictured, and decided on a woman named Roxanne. She had a mature haircut that Thomas had never seen worn by anyone younger than 30 years and her breasts appeared to have been surgically enhanced. Thomas dialed the agency, requested Roxanne and communicated his location.

The author will allow the reader the liberty of determining the psychology behind his choice in a female type that countered his predilection.

Thomas waited an hour before Roxanne arrived. When he answered the door, he was shocked to find that she was more appealing in person.

"Good evening, Thomas," Roxanne said, doting on him with her bedroom eyes.

Her lips were wet and pink with gloss, her eyes shadowed and her cheeks blushed. Around her torso was a white fur coat, and she wore dark denim with red open-toe heels. The angles on her face were sharp, her cheekbones pronounced.

"Good evening, Roxanne. I will be paying in cash," Thomas said.

He reached into his jacket pocket and then set a number of bills on the dresser, including the money Paul had gifted him.

"Your agency already told me the rates, and I know what I want you for and for how long. The money's all there. Come in."

"Mmm," Roxanne moaned. "I like a man who knows exactly what he wants."

Roxanne walked toward the desk in the corner of the hotel room, removed her coat and placed it on the office chair.

Thomas followed her to the desk.

"Don't think I haven't been thinking about it while you kept me waiting."

He fondled Roxanne with greedy hands as he negotiated with her shirt.

"Easy, boy," Roxanne said, gasping as Thomas kissed her neck and ran his hands around her chest and thighs.

"Don't call me boy."

Roxanne giggled.

"But you're younger than me."

"You won't be calling me boy after I'm done with you."

He grabbed Roxanne's shoulders and turned her around so she faced him. He unbuttoned her jeans and put one hand around her throat and the other down her pants. He licked her cold skin, which was studded with gooseflesh, from the side of her neck and up to her ear.

"Do you have any idea what I am going to do to you?" Thomas whispered.

"Oh, God, you're not one of those crazy serial killers, are you?"

"Maybe I am."

Roxanne smiled, purring slightly.

He began removing Roxanne's clothes as the two pressed their hips against one another.

"I promise I won't hurt you any more than you're okay with, but I want to hear you struggle to breathe. I want you to panic. I want to see fear on your face. You can pretend. I'm not going to hurt you. I just want you to act afraid of me."

Thomas had removed both of their clothes. His hands glided along Roxanne's nude figure with such frenzy and force that Roxanne's desire began to drip down her thighs.

"Now be a brave little girl and let Daddy know when he can take control."

"Just do it already," Roxanne shouted.

Thomas pushed her with all of his strength onto the bed. He flexed his muscles as he walked toward her. Thomas twisted her onto her stomach, and eased himself slowly inside of her, leaned over and whispered into her ear.

"I want to strangle you, Bianca. I want to watch you die. You and your fucking father."

Thomas had stayed in the same hotel for an entire week. He figured he would be expected back home and so gathered the belongings he had packed and checked out early in the morning.

On his way out from the hotel, he walked toward the line on the front drive to take a cab home.

"Good morning, sir."

"Hey, Cervantes. How the hell are ya?"

"Very good, my friend."

Thomas had not noticed before how heavy Cervantes'

Mexican accent was.

"Listen, I have something to tell you."

Thomas raised his brow in expectation.

"I want to thank you for what you said to the manager. Because of you, I've been nominated for a Bravo award."

"A Bravo award?"

"Yes, my friend. Every year they hold nominations, and only four employees will win. If I receive the award, I'll win a trip to Italy. The hotel and flight will be paid for and I'll win two-thousand dollars in spending money. It's not often an employee who is not a director or manager is nominated. Even if I don't win the Bravo I am still invited to the banquet and will receive an award. I just want to tell you thanks and that I really appreciate what you've done."

"Well, hey, it was no problem."

Thomas patted Cervantes on the back.

"I hope you get it."

Cervantes blushed slightly, although it was masked by his dark complexion.

"I hope I do, too. My wife and I haven't been on a vacation since we had our first child six years ago."

Thomas once again raised his brow to express his incredulity.

"Well, damn. You deserve it."

"Thanks again, my friend."

Cervantes whistled to signal the next cab in line to approach. He placed Thomas' luggage in the trunk of the cab.

Thomas extended his hand. Cervantes disregarded his gesture and embraced him.

"Take care, my friend," Cervantes said.

"You, too, buddy."

The cab departed for Ray's house. Thomas reflected on the prior occurrence and smiled. His words were insignificant and simple. What was a mere compliment to Cervantes' employers was a grandiose gesture to Cervantes. But the more he thought about it, the more Thomas felt a slight discomfort. His stomach turned. It felt similar to nervousness, but different. Perhaps, Thomas thought, this was the emotional afterglow one receives after performing charity work. These were feelings unfamiliar to Thomas, but he welcomed them regardless.

Thomas retrieved a blank leaf of paper from his briefcase and composed a note relaying to the hotel managers his awareness of Cervantes' Bravo nomination and a list of reasons and an accompanying essay explaining why Cervantes should be one of four employees to receive the award. When he finished he felt as though he had been the one to receive a distinguishing award. He would post the letter when he returned home.

He had done well to neglect considering his issues with Bianca, instead devoting his time to pursuing pleasures that his accountability to Bianca prevented. For example, Asja and Thomas visited one another each day before his leisure time came to an end. Now that his seven days out were over, he thought that he would pay Paul a visit to see how he had been getting on, if he and Tabitha had gotten anything going. He figured it best to, at the very least, discuss his current issues with Paul in order to prepare him for the inevitable discussion with Bianca following his return home.

When Thomas had entered Paul's apartment complex, he thought it odd that nobody was outside as there were usually numerous groups of friends and relatives outside of certain apartments. Thomas knocked on Paul's door four times before Paul came to open it.

"Good, uh...," Paul started.

He laughed in an odd way.

"Good morning, friend."

"Good God, Paul. What happened?"

"The secret, my friend," Paul answered, prodding his finger into his temple.

"What secret?"

"The secret to life. Why, uh...how come you didn't...you didn't tell me before? Ha-ha, it was so easy."

"What in the hell are you on about, Paul? Are you drunk?"

"I am...I'm enlightened. Life starts now," Paul said, slurring. "I mean...I'm talking about my real life. Not this...this, um... delusion, or illusion. It's all a dream. You know?"

"Oh God, Paul, I've turned you into an alcoholic."

Thomas walked into Paul's apartment and took a seat on the recliner.

"Jesus, man. This place is a war zone."

"Don't...now don't...okay, stop being critical. Everything is fine. You just need to relax."

He had never spoken to Thomas with anything more commanding than a suggestion, and this new tone Paul had adopted in his drunken stupor shocked Thomas.

"No, I'm not going to relax. This place has gotten so much worse. It took almost a year for this place to look as trashed as it was seven days ago. In a week's time, you've managed to make it almost twice as bad as it was before."

Paul laughed as though everything were inconsequential. He held his bottle of whiskey before Thomas.

"Here, here. Take this. It's medicine and it will heal you."

"You need to take a look at yourself, Paul, and see what you are becoming. This isn't helping. This shit...."

Thomas tore the bottle from Paul's hand.

"This shit is poison. It will ruin your life if you aren't careful."

"No, no," Paul said, laughing. "Take a look at you. Open your eyes. I understand now. This...everything, it's just...none of it matters. I see that now. All of this, th-this mess, a nice house, everyone...everything outside from here—none of it...it's all nothing. It's all disappeared and I'm...I'm free."

"Paul, honestly, what happened to you? Is this because of something that happened with Tabitha?"

"Tabitha? I haven't...I never called her, you know?"

He boomed with laughter once more.

"I don't need a girl. I'm talking to you. I'm trying to be serious with you. You need...okay, you need to listen. Here is the secret one more time: nothing is the...nothing matters. I'm so happy, Thomas. No more sadness. I'm finished with that. It has always not ever mattered. Do you know that? It hasn't ever—"

"Paul!"

Thomas grabbed his raving mad friend by his dainty shoulders.

"You need to stop this. It's not healthy. There are things that matter in this life."

Thomas reflected on his inauthenticity as he spoke. It was his own carefree attitude which Paul had adopted, although Paul knew no discipline when it came to managing his newfound vice. Thomas' life was a series of inconsequential coincidences, the results of which contributed to nothing greater nor lesser. He saw value in neither death nor life and perceived no worth in those who chose either, yet Thomas felt it necessary to lie, to put on an act for his friend.

"Tabitha...any woman could have changed you for the better. You've chosen this poison and you can't even see that you're falling apart. Paul, your eyes are swollen, your face is bright red, your eyes look bruised from sleep deprivation. You're so bloated that you look like you've gained ten pounds. Your breath smells awful and the city dump keeps a nicer place than you do."

"Ha-ha, fuck you, Thomas," Paul said. "You don't get it. I've figured it out."

Thomas hooked Paul in the mouth. Paul fell to the floor and winced as he ran his hand along his wounded jaw. Thomas then grabbed an open bottle of liquor off of the coffee table and poured the contents over Paul's face. Paul spat and squirmed, struggling to breathe through the flowing liquor that burned his nostrils as it splashed down the bridge of his nose and dripped down the back of his throat and into his sinuses. Thomas then grabbed Paul by the collar and spat in his face.

"No, fuck you, Paul. You're worthless. You're a piece of shit, you know that? You're no better than the fucking trash you've kept in this hole for months. Even the rats won't set foot in here, and you live in this filth. No woman will ever want anything to do with you. You're ugly, you're stupid, you're weak and you have absolutely nothing going for you. You will never accomplish anything in your life aside from lasting seventy or so years living your miserable, lonely life. Then you will die, and nothing happens after that."

Thomas let go of Paul and walked into the kitchen and poured the alcohol out of every bottle that was scattered about. Paul struggled to stand on his feet and stood still in shock as he watched Thomas empty the bottles.

Thomas then spoke with his back turned to Paul.

"If this is how things are going to be, I don't need you anymore. You're useless to me, do you understand? We're finished. You can live the rest of your life utterly and truly alone. How do you think your mother would feel about the life you've chosen for yourself?"

When Thomas had finished emptying the final bottle, he threw it across the room, whereafter it shattered on Paul's closed bedroom door, leaving a large gash in the cheap hollow wood. Paul said nothing and, as Thomas passed, he thought he noticed tears in Paul's eyes, but his tears were as mute as Paul himself. They spoke not a word to Thomas' conscience.

Thomas grabbed the handle of his suitcase and opened the apartment door. He stepped out and, before shutting the door behind him, turned to Paul.

"I'm glad you've got everything figured out, buddy. Goodbye."

Thomas, as he walked home, wondered how he would develop an alibi so he could continue to rendezvous with Asja from then on without Paul's help. Of course, it was possible that he and Bianca were finished, that she had, in the week's time, not reasoned otherwise. If that were so, Thomas, pleased at the thought, imagined himself, free of accountability, engaging in sexual activity with any woman at his leisure, no longer having to settle for rushed licentious affairs.

Bianca never made Thomas feel handsome. His confidence and self-esteem was nurtured by women who did not know him as intimately as Bianca did. Thomas reflected on the nature of monogamy, postulating that it transgressed man's nature. Men were called to conquer and to rule, to exercise strict authority over their dominion and to protect it at any cost. Women should remain man's dominion, Thomas reasoned, not one woman, nor should a man ever, under any circumstances, be any woman's dominion. The weak were fit to be subdued and forced to submit to the strong. To the weak could be granted the displeasures of monogamy for they are too timid and cowardly to acknowledge their nature and accord themselves what could be rightfully theirs, Thomas thought. *Let the bastards bind themselves to a single woman.*

Thomas imagined the course of the discussion he would have with Bianca upon his return. It was quite probable that their conversation would inevitably lead to his exile once again, taking off with the rest of his things and heading downtown where he would store his luggage in a locker in the city's tram terminal and go on to meet Asja. He then began fantasizing about raping Bianca following their heated argument. Ray would listen from his bedroom, too frail and helpless to aid in his daughter's rescue. The scene escalated in violence as he fantasized without restraint; the fantasy punctuated by Bianca lying limp and shivering in her bloodied, ripped clothing.

Thomas rapped quietly on the door when he arrived. It took some time for Bianca to answer and, once she did, she opened it slowly, revealing the pale corpse of the woman he loved.

"Hey," Bianca said softly.

"Hey. Is everything alright? You don't look too well. How have you been doing?"

When Thomas spoke, he expected vitriol from Bianca and wished he had chosen his words with more care.

She sounded like she was moments away from falling asleep.

"I'm not doing well, Thomas. Things are getting worse. I could have used your help."

Thomas entered the house and walked toward the guest bedroom, beckoning Bianca to follow him.

"Where did you go?"

"I stayed at The Plaza," Thomas answered. "They've got decent rooms."

"How was it?"

"You shouldn't have kicked me out if you could have used my help because my point was that you need my help."

Bianca cast her crestfallen eyes on her untrimmed toenails and sighed.

"I know. I'm sorry. I feel like I'm losing everything, like my life is falling apart, and sometimes I feel like you're not there for me when I really need you to be."

Thomas halted his unpacking and walked up to Bianca and

wrapped her in a tight embrace. He kissed her forehead and brushed a stray lock of hair behind her right ear.

"I'm here now, Bianca, and I won't be going away even if you demand that I leave."

Bianca smiled and nestled into his chest. They stood as such in silence for one minute before Thomas heard what sounded like her sniffling.

"Are you crying?"

Bianca grabbed his shirt sleeves and took some moments to compose herself to be able to speak.

"Please don't ever leave me, Thomas," she whispered. "Even if I tell you to."

"I won't, Bianca. I'm here for good."

"Promise me."

Her wet, reddened eyes, the lids drooping from exhaustion, were imbued with a despondence that unnerved Thomas.

"Promise that you won't ever leave me."

"I promise."

She ran her hands down the sleeves of his shirt.

"I need you, Thomas."

"Everything will be alright. I'm here for you now."

CHAPTER NINE

A final encounter with Ray before his death.

In recent weeks, Ray's mental and physical health had steadily declined, a circumstance that Bianca had expected to manifest sooner, although it was a circumstance that, once realized, was more conducive to her despair than the days she spent worried sick over her father's poor condition. Uncertainty, in this case, was like an expected gift-bearer arriving with empty hands–the absence of a gift was a gift in itself. But she was devastated by certainty's essential fulfillment.

She felt blessed to have Thomas to depend on during her trial, and he remained strong and sympathetic to and for her, surprising her with his newfound patience and kindness toward Ray. His improvements touched her heart. This allowed for a closeness between the couple that they had not experienced since moving into the gloomy home. Ray had, as expected, become increasingly critical of Thomas and groaned in protest were Thomas to so much as show his face around him. Thomas would be barraged with insults and profanities as he assisted Bianca with her care-taking duties, but he remained steadfast in his strong stolidity. She would look upon Thomas with admiration as he maintained his composure amidst Ray's abuse.

"You're marrying a fuckin' lousy good-fer-nothin' piece of shit. He's a shit stain."

"Not as rotten as the ones in your drawers, Father," Thomas replied.

Thomas had assumed the habit of ironically calling Ray "Father," wielded as a diminutive in these cases. Bianca had to turn her head when Thomas was getting wise with her father so that she could hide her laughter. Thomas' humorous antics allowed her the privelege of humor despite the tragedy of age on Ray's frail body. Though this indiscretion did leave her feeling somewhat guilty at times, she was appreciative of Thomas' lightheartedness in his dealing with her father as it allowed for a relief, a distraction from an otherwise overwhelming feeling of despair, and his humor countered the strict earnestness with which she handled the affair on her own.

Bianca had developed a mild distaste for her father's company, a predilection that she would not acknowledge to herself, that she possibly was unaware even existed, following his violent shift in mood. She had little patience for his terrible treatment of Thomas, to whom she had bequeathed the unspoken liberty of retaliation. Of course—does it even need stating on behalf of a father's daughter?—she still retained an immortal love for her father.

"Why, you worthless prick. Did your whore of a mother teach you no manners? You ought to respect my authority, ya fuckin' brat."

"Be nice now, Father. You ought to respect the man who changes the plastic sheets you soil every night, lest he may leave you lying in them all through the night."

Ray merely grumbled and raised his voice just enough for Thomas to register the odd curse. Bianca left the room to dispose of the previous night's plastic sheets while Thomas replaced them with a new set. Ray had been turned in his wheelchair to face Thomas.

"I don't need no goddamn doctor, nurse, or pill-pusher to take care of me. Why couldn't ya leave well enough alone? Why can't ya leave Bianca to take care of me? I don't need you and neither does she. She don't even love you anyhow, boy. She told me herself."

"Bianca," Thomas yelled.

After she answered his call he asked that she move his clothes from the washer into the dryer. This, of course, was done to ensure Bianca would not catch him confronting her father.

"Sure," she yelled back.

Thomas then approached Ray, asserting himself inches from his face and spoke thus:

"Ray, look at yourself. Skin and bones is all that remains of the man you once were. You look like you're melting. I could break you with a simple squeeze. Did you imagine that you would be this miserable, that you would be so weak and delicate in your old age? Could you have ever imagined dying to be so dreadful, so boring? You're an old man, Ray, and you need my help after you piss or shit in your pants, after you throw up all over yourself. Imagine a healthy young man's disgust at a much older man's nausea, at the sight of an aged, withered corpse covered in and leaking fluids as you are. You can be certain of this: you are going to die soon, and your precious daughter will belong only to me, and as she leans her head on my shoulder to turn away from your casket as it's lowered into dirt, crying on my shoulder while I watch as you descend into the earth, I hope that you will look up from your miserable hole in Hell to see me smiling. Later that night, do you know what we will do? We're going to fuck, Ray. Afterwards, we'll discuss the terms of our marriage whose ceremony you will not be alive to attend. You will be gone and I will replace you as your daughter's guardian, and I can stop hopelessly wondering what cruel forces were at work which decided that your wife, such a generous and beautiful woman—one whose kindness you did not deserve—should have died before you."

Ray had not broken eye contact with Thomas throughout his diatribe and, although his expression was hardened at first, it softened significantly as Thomas continued. Moisture had begun to leak from cracks in the stone.

"Thomas, what's wrong?" Bianca nearly shouted.

She had addressed Thomas as though he were more capable of determining the state of Ray's health than Ray himself. How, Ray wondered, could anyone but he himself be an authority on his health? Surely he knew what he was feeling for it was he alone that felt it. It was following this consideration that Ray had realized the extent of his existence: it was as a liability, as a burden, as an obstacle that he existed, a pathetic pretense of tendons and bones soon to be disposed of in a small plot on cemetery grounds. Why, then, and how, was he kept alive? His existence was selfish, and the open plot he was destined for was like a chasm, on one side of which Thomas and Bianca stood, and the family they wished to have together on the other. It was necessary for Ray to be buried and fill that chasm so the distance across it could be bridged.

Thomas offered a cartoonish grimace and a shrug of his shoulders in response to Bianca, suggesting that Ray's emotional scene was the ridiculous result of irrationality owing to his age.

"What's wrong?" Bianca then asked her father.

Ray refused a reply. She kneeled down and grasped her father's hands which felt like chapped, wet leather and posed the question once more.

"Please, Dad. You can talk to me."

"I just want to die," Ray answered meekly. "I just want to die. Why can't you let me die?"

"Dad!"

"Just bury me, Bianca. Then you can start a family."

Bianca's tears raced from her eyes as though in competition with her father's.

"I just want to die," Ray repeated.

"Here, you should lie down," Bianca said as she wheeled her father nearer to the bed Thomas had finished preparing.

"Thomas, could you...?"

She stopped short when she noticed that Thomas had already wrapped his arms around Ray's knees.

After they lowered Ray onto his bed, Bianca asked if Thomas could leave the room. Thomas nodded and smiled before turning to leave. He walked into Mary's adjacent garden, strolling slowly by each plant, prodding and stroking the foliage of each as though he wished to sense through the leaves a ghostly trace of Mary's lingering spirit. This garden was the perfect posthumous presentation of Mary, Thomas thought. It was beautiful, elegant, resplendent, marvelous, yet not without an awareness of its own melancholy.

He remembered how overjoyed Mary was over Bianca's engagement to him. She had grown very fond of him and the care with which he treated her daughter, and she would gush when she would see how happy and in love the twosome were. The mood that pervaded their bedroom at present as Ray lie sick in the gloom was too poetic, Thomas thought, considering the emotional tone was befitting of Ray's ugliest qualities, the qualities which most strongly defined his character.

Thomas had made the rounds across the room a dozen or so times, still prodding and stroking the foliage of each plant as he passed, when Bianca had exited the bedroom, shutting the door behind her. Thomas rapped on the wall to catch her attention and, when she turned to face him, he saw her red, swollen face shining with tears. She then ran into Thomas' arms. He wrapped them tight around her torso and under her arms as she had gone limp once in his grasp, then laid her across his lap and supported her with his left arm until she wrapped her arms around his neck, the fabric of his shirt serving to absorb her tears.

"What is it?" Thomas asked with tender conviction.

"He wants to die, Thomas."

Old tears fell anew, adhering to the same moistened path of those that fell before.

"He's sick of living and he wants to die. He told me what pain he's in. He...."

"What?" Thomas asked. "What did he say?"

"He asked me...."

She broke off and shook as she spoke, her voice modulating erratically.

"What did he ask you?" Thomas pressed, becoming impatient.

"He asked me to kill him," she shouted.

She took some time to steel herself before soldiering on.

"He begged me to smother him. He said he would write a note to make it seem like a sucidie, as if that would help to convince me."

A timid *Bianca* was all Thomas could muster.

"You couldn't imagine what it's like to be asked to kill your own father. Imagine the pain he must be in. I can't even imagine tolerating anything close to what he must be enduring. For him to ask his own daughter...."

Thomas smiled as he listened to his sweetheart detail Ray's misery, and, having accepted her pain as a prerequisite to his complete possession and control over her, offered his support and condolences strategically.

"Did he tell you exactly why he wants to…why he feels that way?" Thomas asked, not at all worried whether or not Ray had revealed Thomas' morbid diatribe against him since he knew that Bianca would immediately discount Ray's claims owing to his old age, his insistent hatred of Thomas, as well as Thomas' gracious care of Ray despite the aforementioned. He merely sought amusement and was curious of the old man's explanation.

"He knows that…he thinks that he's standing between us and our starting a family."

Thomas' lips smacked, having opened to agree that Ray was indeed their most considerable obstacle, but he quickly closed them before the words jettisoned from his mouth.

"He is getting closer," Thomas stated, lending an empathetic tone to his words, certain that the ambiguity of his avowal, enrobed as it was in tenderness, would unfurl in Bianca's mind to reveal the ugly nudity of its harsh implication.

"I know, and that is what kills me. I've never really hinted at this—I've always kept it more or less a secret from you—but my dad was very distant when I was a child. I wouldn't really consider him my parent. I mean, he is because he is my biological father, but he never took care of me, and we didn't become close until years later after he suffered his first heart attack. He had to have his first encounter with his own mortality before he really became involved in my life. Here I am heavily involved with and caring exhaustively for a man who never cared for me when I most…when a kid most needs a parent to be a parent. I suppose you could say our relationship is predicated solely by his guilt over being distant from me when I was young. It's funny what bonds people together."

Bianca looked up at Thomas and said, "Could you make

the tea for my dad?"

"Of course, baby."

He laid his hands on her cheeks and kissed her on the lips.

She smiled at him, although in her smile could be intimated a sense of despair. She touched her forehead to Thomas' and sighed.

"I'm going back in there," Bianca said like a soldier addressing their returning to combat. "I need to make sure he doesn't fall asleep before he's had his tea."

Thomas nodded and made off to prepare Ray's beverage, but stopped just before the stairs when Bianca had called his name.

"Yes?"

"Thank you for everything. I don't know what I would do without you. You've been so helpful and patient, and I...."

"That's enough."

Thomas pressed his index finger to his lips.

"You're going to cry yourself dry. It's really no problem. I'd do anything for you, Bianca. I love you."

"I love you, too, Thomas," Bianca muttered behind stifled cries.

Thomas finished brewing the tea and poured it into a mug, inserting five small stirring straws for Ray to sip the tea from. Before he returned upstairs, he walked over to the medicine cabinet and fetched a small vial of eye drops, emptying a few milliliters into Ray's tea before replacing the vial in its usual position. Thomas had gone so far as to leave a right-handed glove hidden atop the cupboards to wear as he handled the vial, and he had traced a faint outline around the bottle so he was able to place it back in its original orientation so that only one's strict vigilance over the amount of fluid left in the bottle coupled with a curiously impertinent suspicion could possibly betray him. Thomas had been routinely poisoning Ray's tea for the last few weeks, tainting just one drink a day every few days, and increasing the volume of poison incrementally each time.

The neurotoxic tetrahydrozoline found in eye drops, when ingested, could result in nausea, seizures, respiratory complications, or even put one in a coma. Ray was neither comatose nor was he experiencing tremors. Instead, he was afflicted by symptoms similar to those of his wife before she had passed from gastroenteritis, although Ray's symptoms following his ingestion of the poison cocktail did not at all rival those Mary experienced following her infection by the norovirus. Ray suffered from vomiting and diarrhea, the latter largely a symptom of his age, and his vomiting was not severe or frequent enough to warrant a doctor's attention. Instead, Bianca relied on Thomas' medical knowledge to care for her father, and he had insisted that his symptoms were relatively normal considering his age and condition.

It had been two days since Thomas had last poisoned Ray's tea. Thomas and Bianca were enjoying a rare instance of each other's intimate company when they heard Ray heaving. Bianca leapt from Thomas as though he were the one heaving, quickly dressed, and ran upstairs. Thomas remained behind to satisfy himself. Bianca returned twenty minutes later.

"He's doing worse and worse as time goes on, and it doesn't get any easier to watch."

"Yeah. He's definitely in a bad way. I could see him going this week."

"Thomas!"

"I don't mean to be insensitive. We just need to be prepared. It could happen at any time."

"You're right. I'm sorry. I just don't want to think about it right now. Could we talk about some–"

She was interrupted by the undulating sounds of her father heaving once more.

"Never mind," she said.

She sighed and left to attend to her father once more.

Thomas laid down to go to bed, teetering on the precipice of waking and sleeping when Bianca returned.

"I don't know that he'll make it much longer. He can't keep his fluids down and there was blood in his vomit. But he's asleep now, hopefully for the night."

"Are you prepared?" Thomas asked.

"Thomas, I could never be prepared to say goodbye to my father."

"That's...yes, I understand, Bianca. Come on, worrying won't change anything. Let's you and I go to bed."

"Anyway, I think it is high time we turn him over to a hospice. I can't do this any more."

Bianca swabbed at her glimmering eyes.

"Give me a second. I'm going to get ready for bed."

For Bianca, her nighttime routine consisted of dosing and sorting numerous medications she had begun to depend on following Ray's decline. She no longer washed her face. Her moisturizers remained capped, and her hair, lately always a mess, looked brittle and dried like the mane of an unwashed mare. She had become a poor sight–her skin had lightened by numerous shades and she was always medicated.

The following morning, Thomas could not wake Bianca from her drugged haze until the mid-afternoon. He returned to their bedroom every quarter of an hour to attempt to wake her once more, and each time she was lying on her side with her mouth agape, saliva running down her cheek and collecting in an ever-expanding wet ring on the sheets–her appearance mirroring death. Thomas decided Ray needed to die before he took the life of his daughter with him and, additionally, before his care was given to a hospice, thus, since he would no longer be poisoned by Thomas' cocktails, possibly extending his life expectancy which would further prolong Bianca's misery.

He walked into the kitchen, climbed on the counter to the immediate right of the kitchen sink and swept his hand over the top of the cupboard until he heard the clink of glass falling over. He took the vial in hand and grabbed the syringe he had left next to it. Thomas then went to shut their bedroom door in the strange case that Bianca would wake and discover his stealthily preparing a major dose of suxamethonium. Once his preparations were complete, he sneaked upstairs, an ordeal that seemed to take ages as the creaking of the old wooden steps sought to betray him at his feet's every impression. Once he reached the top of the stairs, he carefully turned the knob of Ray's bedroom door and threw it open so that the groaning of the hinges would not alert Bianca. He left it open so he would be able to hear if she were to stir.

"Hello, Ray."

The newly awakened Ray turned his head and sunken eyes covered in filmy cataracts upon Thomas, blinking rapidly as his eyes adapted to the sunlight intruding into his somber bedroom from the hallway.

"I've got a surprise for you, Father—something that is going to take the pain away."

Ray was vacant. His gaze remained fixed where Thomas once stood, his mouth fluttering open and shut as though he were speaking, but Ray could vocalize nothing but pained rasps.

"You're making your daughter miserable. Have you seen what a mess you've made of her? Such a selfish old man you are, Father."

Thomas approached Ray's bedside and reached for his arm, but Ray intercepted his wrist and clasped it as hard as his feeble bones could muster and began quietly convulsing as his gaze bore straight into Thomas' soul. His mouth continued to chatter as though he meant to plead with Thomas for relief from mortality. Thomas understood at once the grave implication in the old man's tortured gesture, and rotated his arm so his flowering veins that crept along the pale flesh of his arms like crawling vines on a lattice were exposed.

"This is not going to be easy for you, Father. You've still got a ways to go and it is going to hurt like hell. Your insides are going to burn and your body is going to quake. This is going to deliver the most pain that you will have ever felt in your life. Because of this chemical, you're going to die just like your wife, Ray. You're going to die the death you deserved over her. I should have you know that I've been slowly poisoning your tea more and more in preparation for this exact moment. Your death will seem natural. Nobody will know I was the reason for your death. I'm going to enjoy this, Ray. I've been waiting so patiently to watch you die."

Ray gripped Thomas' wrist ever harder with an unknown force summoned from some instinct whose primitivism defies literary rendering and shook madly as tears streamed down his face. His flapping mouth seemed as though he were crying out, announcing to the heavens, to his departed wife, that he would be with her again soon; to Bianca, that he would be leaving her behind. The bed began shaking with the momentum Ray was generating from his seizure, and Thomas marveled at the passion with which the dying old man was convulsing.

"Goodbye, Ray. Bianca will come to check on you soon. Stay strong enough to say your goodbyes until then."

Thomas administered the dose into Ray's veins and kissed him on his forehead.

"Farewell."

He returned to his and Bianca's bedroom after he had replaced his materials atop the cupboard. He carefully climbed into bed and lay still for some time before he noted a vile odor reeking of feces. Moments later he overheard Ray vomiting.

Bianca did not stir at all as Thomas tried shaking her awake. But she jolted awake when she heard Thomas say, as though in a nightmare, "Bianca, wake up. There's something wrong with Ray."

CHAPTER TEN

End.

Ray had suffered massive trauma and died before the EMT's were able to arrive. Bianca was devastated and in hysterics after witnessing her father pass as violently as he did, keeping her face hidden behind her shaking hands and, when the EMT posed to whomever were to assume the duty of answering–she or Thomas–she would choke on a few struggled syllables before Thomas would offer an intelligible answer.

"Ray's death is not characteristic of those expiring of old age. It seems to have been brought on by something. Did he have any food allergies or allergies to medications, any history of family illness?"

Bianca was only able to answer with a shake of her head, but Thomas interjected as the EMT began making notations on a sheet affixed to his clipboard.

"His wife–her mother–passed due to a severe case of

gastroenteritis. Perhaps it was transmitted."

"Hmm."

The EMT made a notation.

"When did your mother pass?"

Bianca murmured weakly.

"Some months ago," Thomas answered. "While she was on a cruise. It spread among some of the passengers, but she had apparently developed a severe case."

"Okay, and how long had he been exhibiting symptoms?"

"Fuh…fuh…for we—"

Bianca choked on her words.

"For a few weeks," Thomas answered.

Following the conclusion of his note-taking, the EMT lowered his hands to his sides.

"The reason I ask is because, while the norovirus, the viral agent that brings about the symptoms of gastroenteritis, is transmittable, symptoms usually develop anywhere between twelve to seventy-two hours following infection, and the illness is self-limiting, meaning that, even without the aid of medicinal intervention, the illness will usually run its course naturally. In the case of gastroenteritis, this course would be a matter of days, or, at most, nearing two weeks."

Thomas' heart throbbed, and he feared that his physiological response would communicate his guilt. His fear had robbed him of color, a peculiarity that the EMT, with an accusatory raise of an eyebrow and his rigid manner of speaking, conveyed that he had noticed.

"Deaths are relatively rare with cases of gastroenteritis, with only some three hundred cases a year resulting in death, and the fact that Ray had been seemingly struggling with the symptoms for weeks, possibly months, and that it had then ended so dramatically, is very strange."

"Maybe the gastroenteritis weakened his immune system

and he had caught something more serious afterward."

Thomas was concerned that he spoke with an utter lack of conviction.

At the close of the conversation, Bianca had granted her permission for her father's cause of death to be determined through an autopsy. It was not enough to merely know that her father had died. His death, for Bianca, required the proper labels. It needed to be regarded in the proper terms, linguistically dissected and examined. The language of her father's death was equally as important as the knowledge of his death, and she was grateful for the authorized search for the words with which to attribute to her father's passing, unaware that the clamor for vernacular had torn an ideological fissure between her and Thomas. The same language that would ease Bianca, that would lend content and form to a theretofore obfuscated figure by describing exactly what had caused his death, would implicate Thomas, vilify him, deliver him into incarceration.

Thomas had lost to a corpse both feeling and the desire for feeling. His love for Bianca was terminated, all sentiment overridden. After the ambulance left in possession of the hollow vessel that once hosted Ray's spirit, Bianca, in a tragic way and still crying as terribly as if she had just come to learn of her father's death moments ago, invited Thomas back into the house, beckoning to him to be consumed by the darkness inside alongside her forevermore. When he passed through the doorway, he had not entered the same home, or was it that another person entirely had entered a house that was familiar to a consciousness that was no longer his own? The door seemed to creak more miserably than it once did as it closed on the world outside. The stairs groaned sadly under his every step. The bust of Zeus now seemed to scowl upon him with knowing hatred. All of the house seemed to condemn Thomas. Even the temperature, which was much too cold, sought to punish him.

Yes, everything had changed. No longer was anything familiar. Like the brain removed from the home of one's warm skull, wired to electrodes and continuing to operate, albeit absolutely divorced from human context and conceptions of purpose, was Thomas' gray existence—free of context, free of purpose, yet still proceeding onward towards no discernible end.

All shades of conviction, all evocations of affectivity had been at first defaced by the awful splotches of deathly black and blood-soaked red from the mess of Ray's demise. The act of vandalism was then painted over in one grand murderous stroke that colored the canvas stock white, the portrait of his mindscape then becoming absent of all color, appearing as it did before the most minor development, as nondescript and undefined as the consciousness of a newborn child who, through its deficiencies of emotion and reason, are absolutely unable to regard in any manner the vibrant, frenetic world they were born into—tabula rasa restored.

Thomas spoke not one word to Bianca after she collapsed onto his lap in tears, crying out for assurance, begging for pacification, desperate for even the least consolatory gesture. She grabbed and manipulated Thomas' arms into an embrace, but once she relinquished her hold on them they slid down her body and back at his sides. It was as though she were trying to wrap herself in her dead father's embrace.

Bianca, feeling as though she had suffered the death of her love following her father's death, stormed off to sleep, lying in her father's bedstead under sheets that, after having been thoroughly sanitized and thus rinsed of any physical remnant of her father's essence, bore only metaphysical traces of the dearly departed. She could no longer find what she loved of her father in Thomas when the circumstances had strictly begged for those qualities to manifest and be seen. She searched for them elsewhere—in the sheets that had been tightly tucked between the mattress and the box spring to keep Ray from turning on the sides of his brittle bones.

Bianca had spent herself thoroughly through her emotional distress and thus slept heavily, guarded by the fragile illusion of her father's spiritual presence in the room. Meanwhile, Thomas was stuffing his suitcase and duffel bag that, until then, remained symbolically empty—symbols representing permanency whose signification had then been overturned.

After he had finished packing as many accoutrements and provisions as one suitcase and bag could accommodate, additionally taking care in packing the incriminating vial of suxamethonium chloride as well as the used syringe, he did not precede his departure with so much as a tearful tour of the gloomy house. He did not allow himself a final sentimental sauntering through the home he was to prepare for his family-to-be under whose roof his once dearest love was sleeping soundly under. No romantic stroll through memories of the one he was prepared to spend the rest of his life with. No tender kiss upon Bianca's cheek. No farewell.

Not one step did he climb to be able to crack open the door to her father's room in order to peer inside so that he could see her sleeping peacefully before he left her sealed forever within her dreary, miserable tomb. He could see nothing as he walked through the darkened foyer, but he felt his way toward the living room table on which he left the wedding ring he had not yet given her, still embedded in its casing of blue velvet. Thomas then walked outside without ceremony. After locking the door behind him, he threw the key up onto the roof and drove, free to all, on toward nowhere in particular, a cold chill upon his face; bound to nothing, absent from everything.

Thomas drove for miles with his mind occupied with thoughts of the phenomenology of his murder, failing to consider the extant realities of living. He had little money following his week-long vacation and nowhere to stay.

He then started to consider, as he faced the autumnal twilight, where he would seek shelter and how he would obtain the funds suitable both for his escape and for repurposing a life for himself elsewhere. Thomas could not appear at Paul's apartment and beg forgiveness so that he could stay for the night–never mind the insect infestation and the mess–but, Thomas remembered, he had a copy of Paul's apartment key that he had duplicated when Paul had once entrusted his apartment to Thomas.

Thomas travelled to Paul's apartment complex and stalked through the grounds past the dimly lit corridor through which was Paul's door. Standing outside for a few minutes to listen for any sound on the opposite end, he heard only the buzzing of the dim bulb lighting the corridor. He lined his bags against a corner of the corridor wall so they would be unseen by any who may pass and lay a hand on Thomas' belongings before he could return to them.

He detached Paul's key from the keyring so it would not jingle against his other keys and inserted it slowly into the knob. It took Thomas about one minute to turn the unlocked knob as he was careful not to make any noise. He left the door open slightly to allow for an easy exit and stood still for a little while to allow his pupils to dilate so he could make out any possible obstacles. Paul must have been asleep in his bedroom as he was not passed out in the living room as Thomas suspected he would be. He dodged bottles and cups that were strewn about the floor and, after he made it to the kitchen, grabbed Paul's ruined chair and carefully lowered it to the ground. When he went to stand on it, the lopsided chair tipped over and Thomas stumbled back and fell into a cupboard. His body seized with concern and he held his breath to listen for any stirring coming from Paul's bedroom, his body seized with tension like a condensed spring, ready to burst into flight.

He heard nothing.

Climbing atop the chair once more, he reached for the vase, took it in his hands and dumped the money on the counter. Scores of coins spilled out from the vase. Thomas figured that Paul must have been skimming money from his savings for alcohol and dropping the change in the vase. He worried the racket would wake Paul but nothing seemed to disturb him. Thomas pocketed the notes and replaced the chair and figured that Paul must have blacked out. To satisfy his curiosity, he pushed open Paul's bedroom door and saw him lying on the floor.

What a mess, Thomas thought.

His curiosity possessed Thomas to such a degree that he entertained switching on the light for one moment to observe the state Paul and his bedroom were in. Paul always left his bedroom door closed when Thomas was over, and Thomas suspected it was to conceal a mess that surpassed that in his living room. Paul's failure to respond to the noise Thomas had made strengthened his resolve. He felt around for the switch. Once the room became illuminated, he noticed the carpet around Paul had been stained red. For a moment, Thomas figured that it was wine, although he cursed his momentary stupidity when he realized Paul was lying in his own blood.

Thomas looked around his room and marveled at how, aside from a few garments of clothing lying crumpled in odd places, the bedroom was surprisingly clean. He grabbed Paul who was lying on his back, turned him over, keeping his hands away from his face and torso which was wet with blood, and began rummaging through his pockets. He retrieved Paul's keys, his wallet, a number of coins and a folded piece of paper. He leafed through Paul's wallet and pocketed the notes that were inside. He replaced his wallet and keys before unfolding the paper. It was hardly legible as Paul had likely penned it while intoxicated.

It read:

"There's more elsewhere than there is here. I've gone to find it. Goodbye.

"Instructions: please inform an old friend, Thomas Keller, of what happened here. With any luck he will understand the truth. My apologies to no one."

Thomas replaced the note in the front pocket of Paul's jeans and turned him back to the position he found him in. He walked into Paul's kitchen and donned a pair of dishwashing gloves before returning to Paul's room, after which he opened every drawer and cabinet in the bedroom and bathroom, searching anywhere he could think of where something of value could be hidden, but he found nothing save for the occasional collection of crumpled and neglected bills.

Well, that saves me two-hundred and fifty bucks, Thomas joked to himself.

When Thomas was finished rummaging through Paul's things, he took care wiping every surface he had touched with his bare hands so that his fingerprints would not be found. He worried that, were he to neglect one surface, one of his prints would be discovered and thus rule Paul's suicide as a murder, with Thomas judged as the murderer. Once he was satisfied with his attention to the surfaces he had touched earlier, he exited and locked the door, took his bags in hand and decided he would pay Asja a visit. Asja would likely be upset to be awoken at such an hour but Thomas would not mind contending with her attitude if it would earn him one final tryst and a chance to say goodbye.

It was not much later than midnight when he arrived. Thomas wondered if Asja might still be awake. He knocked on the door.

"Good evening, Thomas. What the hell are you doing here this late? Did you and your old lady have a lover's quarrel?"

"Yeah, yeah. You know how it goes."

"Not really. You and I never used to fight when we were dating. You must love her to keep running back to her as much as you do."

"Well," Thomas began, but he said no more.

Asja chuckled and stroked Thomas' cheek.

"Come in if you'd like."

Thomas stepped inside and left his bags near her door.

"So what were you thinking?" Asja asked. "Revenge?"

"Of course I was. You know me so well."

"Come take me, then," Asja stated as she fingered the hem of her nightgown. "I'm your prey."

Thomas snickered.

"Listen, Ajsa, could we take it easy for a little while?"

"Like a date, or something tacky like that?" Asja joked. "Do you want to get to know each other, or something?"

"Why not? We've got the night ahead of us. We're always so quick to rush into things. We have all the time in the world tonight. Let's just relax, have some fun and we can end the night the same way in which we're always so rushed to start the afternoon."

"I suppose we could do that."

"Hold on. I should have a bottle of wine in here I grabbed before I was exiled."

Thomas sorted through his shoulder bag and quickly pocketed a sheet enclosing two small pills.

"No dice. I must have forgotten it."

"Well, you're in luck, pal, because you know I always have enough to make sure nobody ever goes thirsty."

"That's true," Thomas said. "You stay here, doll. I'll be

back with glasses for the two of us."

"Aww, Thomas, you're too sweet. Bianca doesn't know how good she's got it with you."

"Because she doesn't know what's good for her."

Asja laughed. She then stood up and walked towards the turntable. She flipped through her small collection of records and decided on Red Hot and Cool by Dave Brubeck, featuring Paul Desmond. The cover of the album shows a stylish woman in bright red–red dress, lipstick, nails, and cherry earrings. She leans onto the piano Brubeck is playing, a cigarette in hand, and looks at him with an expression that is equal parts flirtatious and playful. Dave radiates exuberance as he shares a laugh with the woman. The lounge, as well as the rest of the band, is out of focus, the focal point of the picture being the twosome. On Dave's ring finger is a wedding ring, and one is likely to believe that the woman in red is not his wife but a wishful suitor.

Thomas returned to the living room with two glasses of sparkling liquid in each hand, and Asja danced towards him to grab her glass. She sipped from the glass as she continued sauntering about.

Thomas noticed the jacket of the album.

"Ah, nice choice."

"You know I can't stand musicians who take themselves so seriously. This is such a fun album, not like the depressing Bill Evans or Mingus numbers that drag on and on."

"You know," Thomas began, grabbing the album's jacket as he danced with Asja. "These two on the cover–that's us."

"How so?"

"Notice the ring, first of all. This woman cannot be his wife. Look how goddamn happy Dave is. He's beaming. This woman is doting over him as he's playing, telling him how great he is, how handsome and creative he is. She's fulfilling him in every way his wife no longer does."

"Go on," Asja said, taking another sip from her glass. "I like where this is going."

Thomas put the jacket down and took a large sip of wine before placing his glass down on the table. He grabbed Asja's empty glass and set it down on one of her speakers. He sauntered over to her, placed one hand around her hip and placed the other firmly in her hand, and they began to dance.

"Essentially, Asja, I'm saying you fulfill many things for me that Bianca does not."

"Oh, Thomas."

She was blushing while she toyed with the engagement ring on his finger.

"That's the sweetest thing you've said to me. Most of the time you're a pig but you sure know how to be charming when it suits you. I've always loved that about you—just the right amount of charm to offset how much of an asshole you are."

Thomas removed his ring and pocketed it. He took Asja in his arms.

"Let me show you just how charming I can be."

He took her down on the couch and made love to her, treating her softly.

"Thomas," Asja moaned. "You've never been so sweet. It's really sexy."

Thomas sucked on her tongue for a moment.

"You're beautiful, Asja."

Asja continued to blush. She gasped in pleasure as Thomas made love to her.

"Do you like me, Thomas? Do you like me as more than a fuck?"

"I wish I could see you more often," Thomas answered. "Do you know how much I miss and think about your gorgeous little body?"

"No, Thomas. I want you to think about me like we're not

having sex."

"But we are."

"I know," Asja said, her brow tensed while her legs shook both from frustration and sexual pleasure.

She squirmed as Thomas took her sex in his mouth.

"If it weren't for Bianca, would you be with me? I mean, would we get back together again?"

"We would," Thomas answered. "But it will probably never happen."

"Why not?"

Asja cast her crestfallen eyes on her lover, although an anamalous moan burst through her wounded features.

"It's not that easy, Asja."

"But I love you, Thomas!"

Thomas halted his lovemaking and gazed into her eyes.

"You're so sexy. I think you're so intelligent, you're mature, you're handsome, you fuck me like no one else, you do things to me nobody has done to me before. I masturbate constantly thinking about the times we've fucked. I miss the way you used to whisper in my ear when we'd make love, the way you used to hold me when we were through, squeezing me until I couldn't breathe. You used to rub the tip of your finger against my lips before you'd kiss me. You'd put your hand on my cheek and stare into my eyes. You used to nestle your nose into my face and my neck like we were animals, like I was your child, and you used to just lie there with your body pressing into mine and you would be pulling my body into yours. I felt like we were truly together. You were usually so rough but there were times you would be so delicate that I would get butterflies in my stomach. No one's ever made me feel that way before, Thomas. I've never felt so close to somebody else, and I've never stopped being in love with you."

"Could we talk about this later? Now isn't the time."

Asja began tearing up.

"No," she shouted. "I know you're going to leave me. You're going to marry that bitch, who doesn't even fucking deserve you, by the way, and move off somewhere else, and then I'll never see you again."

"Asja, please."

Asja's eyes glazed over. Thomas then introduced himself inside of her.

Before either could reach orgasm, she began yawning and soon stopped reacting to his thrusts. She had fallen asleep, but Thomas continued thrusting inside of her until he had satisfied himself. He called out to her, shook her and slapped her face softly to see if she would wake but she did not respond.

Thomas dressed and then made for Asja's bedroom and sorted through her purse. He fetched her wallet and removed the money contained within. When he replaced it, he returned to the living room. He was not going to finger through her belongings. Between Paul and Asja's money, Thomas had net a considerable sum.

He turned the record player and stereo off and placed the record and the enclosing sleeve back into the jacket and filed it in order. On a desk was a pad of lined paper and a container full of pens.

Thomas wrote:

"Dear Asja,

"I am on the run from an organization who may or may not present themselves to you under the pretense of discovering my whereabouts. I have taken some money from your purse–please forgive me. When the time is right I shall return with much more than I took and you and I will run away and start a new life together. Do not forget what has been said tonight–that you have always remained in love with me–and do not forget the tears you shed for me. They were not wasted. I love you, too, but, unfortunately, our time has not yet arrived. I will return to you some time soon, Asja. Wait for me. Keep me alive in your memories and hold me in your heart.

"P.S. It should be obvious, but I will be unable to make good on my promise if I am discovered by the police. Please play your part and deny that I was ever here.

"P.P.S. Do not worry yourself as to why I am evading the law. I have become the victim of false charges which you may or may not become aware of soon (involving Bianca's father, incidentally also the reason we are finished–quite a mess, really). You will see me when my name is cleared, or when the heat dies down. It should be soon as I am an innocent man.

"P.P.P.S. This is quite the possibly incriminating letter. However, I trust your sensitivity with such an issue as this and I have absolute faith in our future together once the knots of this Gordian ordeal are unraveled.

"With love,

"Thomas Keller"

Thomas smirked over the dramatic nature of his letter and his false promise to Asja. He gathered his things and, before he left her house, he pocketed a pack of her cigarettes and a book of matches. Orange splotches of daylight would soon stain the evening sky, and Thomas hoped to skip town before then. He had no idea where he would end up. Whatever the destination, it would be of no consequence to Thomas, to whom each of life's happenings was but an episode in a mortal drama he felt as though he witnessed from a third-party perspective. Every happening in his life, however dreadful or otherwise, was entertainment that he held audience to.

What an interesting day it's been, Thomas thought. *Never mind these last months.*

He smiled to himself as he removed a cigarette from the pack he had lifted from Asja's, struck a match, and held the playful flame before the tobacco. Thomas, having never smoked prior to this episode, coughed after attempting to inhale the smoke.

This is terrible, he said to himself.

Thomas threw the lit cigarette on the ground and stomped on it to extinguish the embers. Once inside his car, he switched on the ignition, and couldn't help another fit of coughs. He laughed at himself.

I'm never trying one of those again.